The Stockade

The Stockade

by *KENNETH LAMOTT*

Little, Brown and Company · *Boston*

Published simultaneously
in Canada by McClelland and Stewart Limited

PRINTED IN THE UNITED STATES OF AMERICA

The Stockade

One

"IT'S a hell of a note," the doctor complained, stopping on the narrow trail. "It seems to me like a hell of a note. They should have sent you people up here a week ago. I'm just a doctor, not a platoon of marines."

Lieutenant Rossi was waiting a few yards ahead of him, showing only a mild impatience. "Somebody always gets the dirty end of the stick," he said evenly. His tall, lean body was clothed in faded dungarees that were coated with a fine yellow dust his sweat had clotted into many dark patches. He was bareheaded, but his close-cropped black hair grew over his forehead like a cap.

The doctor gingerly stroked the tender red skin on the back of his neck. He moved his hand carefully so as to avoid the pale, dime-sized blisters that throbbed in the hot sun. His face was drawn and pouchy, as if the sun had dried out all its fat. A long lock of hair, which was apparently intended to conceal a patch of shining pink scalp, had been blown to one side, where it hung over his temple in a ragged fringe. He was older than Rossi by twenty years or so, and where Rossi was self-possessed, he was harried and distraught.

"Listen to them," the doctor said, looking toward the foot of the hill. The stand of pines below them cut off a view of the stockade but they could hear a thin, indeterminate crowd-sound punctuated by the shrill cries of individual voices. "Five thousand Okinawans and Koreans and God-only-knows-what-all and the goddamn United States Navy sends ashore a doctor and a crazy corpsman. Wouldn't you think *somebody* would know what the score was?"

"The dirty end of the stick," Rossi repeated. He was watching the LSTs and transports that floated on the surface of the bay like toys in a bathtub. Between the bay and the hill were narrow white beaches and green cane fields that carpeted the island from the airstrip on the north to the escarpment on the south.

"This corpsman of mine," the doctor said, "the man's mad. What's *he* doing here? Why should I be marooned with *him* at this godforsaken stockade?"

"Things are tough all over," Rossi said.

"A marine," said the doctor bitterly. "You probably wanted to come on this operation."

"I've seen worse," Rossi said, and turned up the trail.

"*Gung-ho!*" the doctor mocked. "*Semper fi!*"

Rossi shrugged. He was several yards up the trail and had begun to climb in earnest. The doctor followed him.

"Don't think I'm not glad you're here," the doctor said apologetically. "I don't think I would have lasted another week by myself. I've been on the go all day and most of the nights."

Rossi forged ahead without answering and the doctor was forced to quicken his pace. The trail grew narrower and thin, tough wands of brush that bent like springs as Rossi passed lashed back at him. A colony of monstrous black flies that had been clinging to the brush rose and buzzed angrily about the doctor's head. The doctor struck out savagely with his stubby

4

arms against the whiplashes and the insistent flies. He cried for Rossi to stop, but Rossi continued relentlessly toward the summit.

The trail suddenly debouched from the pines and the chest-high brush into a small clearing. The doctor stumbled and pitched forward into the dust, where he crouched for a moment, gasping from his sudden fall, the heat of the day, and the steep climb. He spat into the dust and wiped his cracked lips on the sleeve of the green shirt that clung in damp folds to his chest.

"What the hell's this?" Rossi demanded.

"Psycho ward," the doctor said. He lifted the sodden cloth of his shirt away from his skin to let the air through to where the sweat had raised a prickling red rash. "We built it up here to keep the lunatics away from the rest of the gooks. Our little brown brothers down below had them tied hand and foot when we came. I've done the best I can for them, but it isn't much."

Four poles had been driven into the ground at the corners of a rough rectangle measuring ten paces by five. Around the poles, encircling them and forming a cage, were three strands of barbed wire. A torn, dun-colored tarpaulin was stretched across the cage. It covered half of the enclosed area and fell to the ground on three sides, making a crude tent. In the shade of the tent the lunatics crouched against the wire or lay full-length upon the ground. The unshaded part of the cage was empty except for two C-ration tins that were lying in the dust. There was no entrance or exit except through the wire.

"Who strung that wire?" Rossi asked.

"The doctor did," a voice behind them said. "The doctor and I did."

"Damn it, Loomis, you're supposed to be holding sick call."

"I secured from sick call." Loomis stood slightly apart from the doctor and Rossi, a tall, stooped man in Seabee-issue dungarees and a short-billed baseball cap on which was pinned the anchor of a chief petty officer.

"That tarp," Loomis said to Rossi, "I got from an old Jap supply dump down the road. The poles I cut myself. The doctor and I strung the wire one afternoon. It wouldn't do to keep the hogs in back home but it's good enough for these goddamn gooks."

Loomis went to the cage and shook one of the poles. The whole cage swayed, creakingly. A creature dressed in appallingly filthy rags crawled from under the tarp and squatted by the wire, blinking his red-rimmed eyes in the sunlight. His legs were covered with open sores on which the greedy flies feasted undisturbed. He scrabbled in the dust for one of the tin cans, which he held out to Loomis, croaking at him in a voice like the whine of a saw cutting through knotty lumber.

"That's Smoky Joe. He wants water," Loomis said, "but he's had his water for the day."

"You should have put up more wire," Rossi told the doctor.

"It's all we could get," the doctor said. "It's Jap wire at that."

"If you don't watch out you'll have them running loose all over the stockade."

"They do. Loomis rounds them up in the mornings."

A second man came from the tent. He stood so close to the wire that the barbs seemed about to pierce his flesh. He looked at Loomis and began to laugh. His amusement waned quickly and he sat in the dust, where he picked at the soles of his feet with the ragged points of his fingernails.

"I'll get my men on this cage in the morning," Rossi said. "I guess we'll have to let Loomis round them up for one more night."

"You're going to leave them here?"

"Leave them? What else can I do with them?"

"Get them out of here. Send them somewhere else."

There was a disturbance within the tent. A high-pitched voice complained briefly and then there was quiet again.

"We'll fix the cage so they won't give you any more trouble."

The doctor shook his head stubbornly. "That isn't what I meant at all. As long as you keep them here they're going to raise hell with the whole camp. When they get excited they can kick up a racket that'll keep you up half the night."

"We'll see," Rossi said. "If it gets too bad, we'll have to do something about it." He turned to Loomis. "You're their keeper, Chief. What do you think?"

"I can take care of them," Loomis said. "They don't give me much trouble."

"Much trouble! Oh, my God!" the doctor groaned. The voice from the tent answered, scolding him vigorously.

"What about the ones that get out?" Rossi asked.

Loomis grinned. "The gooks catch them for me. They tie them up and keep them until morning. Then I pick them up and put them back in the cage. Haven't lost one yet."

"You're going to have to get these people out of here," the doctor insisted.

Rossi ignored the doctor. "We'll fix the cage for you. You won't have to chase them any more."

"All right," Loomis said. "I guess that'll be all right."

"Damn it!" the doctor shouted, "I'm the doctor here and I say that they have to go." Rossi and Loomis both turned and looked blankly at him.

"Where?" Rossi asked quietly. "If you think anybody on this island is going to take half a dozen crazy gooks off your hands, you're as crazy as they are."

The doctor's hand explored the mottled skin on his neck. He grunted suddenly with pain and wiped his fingers on his shirt. He took a clean handkerchief from his pocket and pressed it against the broken blister.

"It's only a temporary arrangement," Rossi said. "All I'm interested in is keeping these gooks alive until the military government people get here."

"I suppose you're right," the doctor said at last. "Let's get out of here."

But as he turned to go, Loomis detained him. "Here she comes, Doc."

The doctor saw the woman come from the tent and pad to the center of the cage, where she knelt with her hands folded in her lap. A young girl followed her. The girl scooped up a handful of dust and held it out to the woman, who dipped her hands in the dust, closed her eyes, and stroked the dust carefully over her face. When she was through, the powdery dust covered her face in a thick, even layer.

"*Chan-chan-chan*," sang the girl, "*cha-a-an, cha-a-an, chan-chan-chan*." While she sang she plucked at an imaginary stringed instrument that was cradled in her lap. The two men inside the cage turned to watch.

The woman rose slowly and gracefully. She stood quietly for a moment, her face as gray and unlined and lifeless as if it had been molded of clay. Then she began to dance. She used her body, which was as supple as a reed of young bamboo, with deliberate and stately artistry. She raised her arms and opened an imaginary fan, and the torn gold threads on her kimono

8

glinted in the sunlight. While the girl chanted, the dancer sang in a high, clear voice, a song of spring and the cherry blossoms, or of the moon reflected in Lake Biwa, or of a soldier come home from the wars.

"A gee-sha girl," Rossi said. "What's she doing in there?"

The doctor didn't answer. He was watching the dancer attentively, as if he were awaiting the manifestation of the clinical symptoms of her disease. But the dancer was in complete control of her performance. Her voice remained high but sweet and her body executed the formal patterns of the dance with the seemingly effortless precision of the professional. Her face revealed that she was utterly oblivious of her audience.

Suddenly one of the men inside the cage rose to his feet and hurled his water can at the dancer. It arched over her shoulder and clattered against the wire at the far side of the cage.

"Aaaaaaaaaaaah-ah!" screamed the dancer and the imaginary fan that had shaded her face fell to the ground. She stood twisted in the attitude of the dance, her slim, tapering hands shielding her face. Only the accompanist moved, plucking tirelessly at her nonexistent samisen.

"Let's go," the doctor said. "Let's go, Lieutenant."

"*Chan-chan-chan-chan-chan-chan-chan-chan-chan.*"

The dancer stamped on the ground and the dust rose and settled on her gold-embroidered kimono.

"Let's go," the doctor pleaded. His throat was dry and a sour bile taste flooded his mouth. He grasped Rossi by the arm. "Come on, Lieutenant."

But Rossi and Loomis remained by the cage, waiting. The doctor started down the trail alone. At first he made his way cautiously, but he was running like the wind when he heard the first wild shriek that echoed over the plain below.

9

Two

SWENSON, Lieutenant Rossi's platoon sergeant, walked toward the square that was in the center of the stockade, swinging at his side the club he had shaped from a piece of wood salvaged from the litter behind his hut. The haft of the club was ridged with neatly carved grooves and fitted solidly in his big fist. Swenson swung the club lightly into the open palm of his left hand and felt his skin tingle at the sharp impact. Swenson had acquired a partiality for clubs when, as a pfc on guard duty at the brig at Pearl, he had unintentionally fractured a prisoner's skull. The boy was waiting to be tried for desertion and the official report had said that he had stumbled and cracked his skull against a wall while double-timing it to the head. Swenson had never thought of himself as a brutal man and the incident had surprised him even more than it had the unlucky seaman. At the same time Swenson was not averse to developing a new skill, which he was always careful to exercise only in the line of duty. It was only after Swenson's growing virtuosity had become an embarrassment to his superiors that he had been transferred to the Fleet.

The children who had been playing in the road slipped under the wire and followed Swenson to the square, which was dense with the prisoners, swarming like maggots on a dusty carcass.

The warm breeze that blew off the mountain brought to Swenson a rancid odor of sweat and decay, a musty reminder of dank, airless caves. Mingled with it was something not unlike the sweet, heavy stink of a week-old corpse. Swenson hawked loudly and spat on the ground.

A hoarse cry went up near him and for a moment motion hung suspended in the square. Two rusty sheets of corrugated iron were dropped to the ground and crashed out an alarm. A woman drawing water at the well let the water overflow her pail and make a dark streak of mud in the dust. Then, as quickly as they had taken alarm, the prisoners left their work and closed in on Swenson in a semicircle. The children who had followed him fanned out behind him and Swenson was completely surrounded.

Swenson remained for a moment on the edge of the square, an old excitement quickening within him, and then he grasped his club firmly and marched into the semicircle. The prisoners fell away and formed a wide lane for him. Swenson marched ahead slowly, scanning the faces on either side.

"You!" he commanded.

A scrawny man wearing a warped stiff straw hat struggled to push his way back into the crowd but the line held as firmly as if the onlookers were in collusion with Swenson.

"Take off that hat when you see me coming."

The man gibbered in terror and plucked at his open shirt with trembling fingers. Swenson brought his club up sharply and flicked the straw hat into the air. It twisted end-over-end and fell into the crowd.

"Savvy?"

Swenson's victim laughed shrilly. He bobbed his head up and down and grimaced grotesquely while he tried to subdue the crazy laughter that had taken hold of him. Swenson pointed the blunt end of the club into the man's stomach, into the spot where the lowest ribs form an inverted V, and pushed expertly. The wood probed the tense muscles and the victim gasped and toppled into the space that had suddenly opened up behind him.

Swenson swung away and continued across the square and into the trees.

None of the prisoners followed him and the huts among the trees seemed to be deserted except for a band of boys around a hut. They were trying to capture a spotted puppy that had crawled between the floor and the ground. The oldest of the boys grabbed the puppy by the tail but the little animal squealed and snapped at his hand and escaped further into the darkness underneath the floor. The boys surrounded the house and crawled toward the puppy from three sides, driving him toward their leader, who shouted in triumph and caught the puppy by the neck. He held it aloft, his small hand firmly clutching the struggling puppy. The puppy squealed and shook and then hung limply while the children gathered around and grinned.

"That's no way to treat a pup," Swenson said sternly. "Put him down."

The oldest boy dropped his arm to his side but retained his hold on the puppy, which renewed its struggling.

"Let him go!" Swenson bellowed.

The boy dropped the puppy, which scrambled to its feet and ran panting to its refuge underneath the hut. The boys ringed Swenson and stared at him curiously. They began to chatter among themselves, pointing at various items of Swenson's equipment.

"Knock that stuff off," Swenson said angrily. "Don't you

goddamn gook kids mess around with that pup. He hasn't done you no harm."

The oldest boy brazenly put out his hand. "*Shigaretto*," he demanded.

"Go to hell," Swenson said. "You're not old enough to smoke, you goddamn little gook."

The boy came nearer.

"*Shigaretto*," he whined, "*tabako*."

Swenson made a motion as if he were going to strike him on the rump but stopped abruptly. A girl carrying two heavy pails of water had come around the corner of the hut. When she saw Swenson she dropped her pails to the ground and stood still for a moment, her round, peasant face surprised and frightened. The points of her full breasts showed through the thin material of her dress and when she turned to flee her skirt clung tightly to her plump thighs. Swenson followed her behind the hut but she was gone. He looked through a window into the single room inside. A shaft of light came through a hole in the roof the size of a man's head and fell on a pile of cloth-wrapped bundles heaped in a corner. The bundles were lumpy and showed the outlines of cook pots and small pieces of household furniture. In a dark corner of the room an old woman, swathed in a dark garment, lay on a pile of torn quilts. She grumbled querulously at Swenson.

"Where'd the girl go?" Swenson asked. The old woman turned her face to the wall. Swenson repeated his question. The woman groaned and drew her clothing more closely about her.

Swenson completed his circuit of the hut and then went on up the path. The boys followed him until one of them discovered that a pot of cooked rice had been left unguarded in

13

front of a hut. They fell on the pot and scooped out the glutinous grains with their dirty hands.

The well at the end of the path was shaded by two immense, gnarled trees. The stone side of the well had fallen in and the well was half filled with earth and stones. Swenson stood in the shade of the trees and peered down the shaft. A frog leaped from the earthy slope and splashed into the muddy pool at the bottom. Swenson lighted a cigarette and sat in the shade while he considered the ways and means of restoring the well, and other matters that were on his mind. After a while he ground out his cigarette and went back down the path.

The prisoners were at their huts preparing their evening meals. Swenson stopped at the hut where he had seen the girl. The boys had not returned but an old man wearing a shapeless felt hat was sitting in the doorway smoking a long-stemmed pipe with a tiny brass bowl. He looked at Swenson without interest. The old woman moaned inside and the voice of a young girl answered her. There was a rustle of bedding being moved and then the girl came out and put a handful of greens into a pot that was boiling over an open fire in the dooryard. The girl ignored Swenson and stirred the mixture in the pot. As she bent over her work Swenson could see the swell of her breasts through the open neck of her dress. The old man knocked the dottle from his pipe and refilled it with a pinch of tobacco from a small enameled case.

Swenson took a bar of tropical chocolate from the pocket of his dungaree jacket and held it out to the girl.

"Here," he said, "for you."

The old man stared at him blankly and the girl turned her back and busied herself with the cooking.

"It's chocolate. I'm not going to hurt you."

14

The old man spoke to the girl and she came forward and took the chocolate, but she was frightened and ran back immediately to the cook pot. Swenson followed her.

"What's cooking?" he asked amiably.

The girl kept her head averted and drew away from him. Swenson reached out to touch her bare arm.

"No," the old man said, "no good."

"You speak English?"

"Sure. Live Hilo five years. Ask doctor. Kaneshiro."

"What the hell's Kaneshiro?"

The old man pointed to his chest. "Me."

"Well now, look here. Is that girl your daughter?"

"No," Kaneshiro repeated, "no good."

"I'm just trying to be friendly," Swenson said. "I'll tell you if she's any good or not."

Kaneshiro spoke to the girl and she ran into the hut. Swenson advanced on the old man, smacking his club into the palm of his hand.

"Now look here, you old buzzard — "

Kaneshiro stared back coolly and puffed on his pipe. Swenson was about to shove him out of the way when the old man took the pipe from his mouth.

"Cigarette," he said.

"Ah, hell, is that all you wanted." Swenson dug into his pocket and pulled out a crumpled cigarette. The old man took it and ripped the paper lengthwise. He dropped the loose tobacco into his tobacco case. He continued to block the doorway.

"Out of my way. Chop-chop!"

Kaneshiro rocked on his heels and grinned. "Whisky," he said.

"Whisky? What the hell do you mean, whisky?"

The old man called to the girl, who brought out a square bottle and two dirty teacups without handles and placed them on the floor. Kaneshiro uncorked the bottle and poured an inch of yellow liquor into each cup. Swenson sniffed at the liquor and then gulped it down.

"Whisky!" he sputtered. "Jesus Kee-rist!" He shuddered and wiped his lips. Kaneshiro corked the bottle and handed it to the girl with a shrug.

"Well now," Swenson said, "I don't mind if I do have a bit more." He held out his empty cup and the girl uncorked the bottle. She sat on her haunches with the bottle in one hand and Swenson's cup in the other and measured off three quarters of a cup.

"Bottoms up," Kaneshiro said, raising his cup to his lips.

"Sure," Swenson said, and tossed off his drink. "Now let's talk business."

Three

THE huts across the road were larger and sturdier than those in the stockade. In the old days the foremen had lived by the road and the field workers in the huts up the mountain. Now the foremen's quarters were occupied by the marines. A clump of trees shaded the road and the hut which Swenson shared with Sergeant Taliaferro, across from the doctor and Rossi. The rest of the men lived in the long, low shed that stretched out behind Swenson's hut. Loomis lived alone in a shack that had once been used as a tool shed.

The largest hut really consisted of only one room, but a long closet filled with moldy-smelling bedding extended halfway across, separating Rossi's cubicle from the doctor's. A burst of machine-gun fire from a fighter plane had ripped holes in the tin roof, but these had been covered with more tin and when it rained, as it did almost every night, the water flowed into the gutters and down a drainpipe to the concrete cistern in back.

Rossi was cleaning his carbine in the light of a candle fixed to an empty ration can. The stock, detached from the barrel and looking like a crudely made child's toy, lay on the cot. Rossi was running a clean patch through the bore when the doctor came into the room and stood by the closet, watching him. Rossi fitted the gun together, slipping the parts into place

17

quickly and easily. Finally he tightened the steel band that holds the barrel to the stock, and snapped the magazine into place.

The doctor came closer. "How do you think you're going to like it here?"

The room was small, clean, and bare. Rossi's pistol belt and helmet hung from nails on the wall behind the cot, which was the only piece of furniture. There was a field pack on the wall at the head of the cot. Rossi hung the carbine on a nail next to the pistol belt.

"It'll do. I've slept in a lot worse places."

"You'd better use your net. The mosquitoes can become pretty fierce."

"I know." Rossi pulled back the sleeve of his jacket and showed the doctor the red welts that ran up his arm. "We slept out in the boondocks last night. Damn near got eaten alive."

"You have to watch out for dengue," the doctor said. "It doesn't hang on like malaria, but it'll make you think you've broken every bone in your body."

"I've had it twice."

The doctor stood uneasily in the center of the room, nervously rubbing the back of his neck.

"How about a drink?" he said at last.

"Thanks. I could use one."

The doctor went to his room and came back with a quart bottle. He handed it to Rossi, who held it up to the light of the candle. The liquid in the bottle was pale yellow and faintly cloudy. The label showed two faded green palm trees framing a yellow sailing ship on a purple sea. Underneath the trees was the legend: BESST QALITY RUM, and a line of Japanese characters. Rossi pulled out the wad of paper that served as a cork and sniffed.

18

"It doesn't smell much like rum," he said dubiously, but he took his canteen cup from the wall and was preparing to fill it when the doctor snatched the bottle from him.

The doctor went to his room and returned with a white enamel hospital can and a handful of tinfoil packets of synthetic lemon powder. He mixed the powder with water from Rossi's canteen and then added a large slug of rum. He tasted it and added more rum.

"It's all right," he announced at last. "As a matter of fact, it's not bad at all." He poured half the liquid into the canteen cup and gave it to Rossi. Rossi lighted a cigarette and lay full length on his cot, balancing the cup on his chest. The doctor pulled a heavy quilt from the closet and made a rough couch of it against the wall.

The window at the foot of Rossi's cot faced the stockade. There was no moon and Rossi could see only a few leaves that rustled against the window sill. They were withered and dead-looking in the pale light of the candle. A low, almost inaudible sound came from the stockade.

"Lord," the doctor said, "I was really wound up this afternoon. The dancer was the last straw." He watched Rossi intently.

"We all get that way sometimes," Rossi said, but there was no sympathy in his voice. "Does that dancer put on her act very often?"

"You'll probably hear her every night, just about the time you want to hit the sack."

"Nothing you can do about her?"

"Treatment? No, not here at any rate."

"She looked as if she might have been pretty good before she cracked up."

"I imagine she was."

"What about the others in the cage?"

"They're like the men you saw. Fortunately, none of them are likely to get really violent."

"The thing I can't understand is how you tell the crazy ones from the rest. These gooks all look sort of nuts to me."

"Oh, no," the doctor protested earnestly. "Actually, these Okinawans are a pretty stable race. When you consider what they've been through — "

"They're still gooks."

"Well, you're going to have to get along with them for a while. You may not like them, but, after all, your men are probably a lot more comfortable than they've been for quite a while."

"Too damn comfortable. I don't like this setup at all. I think I have a pretty fair platoon, what's left of it, but we've been out here too long. Some of the men, Swenson and Taliaferro for instance, haven't had a piece of tail for over a year. How do you expect them to act if you put them in charge of a couple thousand women, even if they *are* gooks? I'd rather they'd kept us down south until they were ready to ship us back to Maui. We might have lost a couple more men but I'd rather take a chance on that than see the whole platoon rot away in this hole."

The doctor said nothing. He took a long drink and brushed some stray cigarette ashes from his shirt.

"Tell me about these gooks," Rossi said. "Where'd they all come from?"

"The Japanese brought most of them from Okinawa to work in the cane fields. They came on three-year contracts, hoping to put away enough money to go home and take it easy, but they stayed on for a number of reasons — they were paid only half the wages they'd been promised, they got in debt to the company, and so forth. Some of them even got to like the island. The rest are Koreans. I don't know what sort of terms they came over on, but judging from the way they look the Japanese must have treated them even worse than they did the Okinawans."

"Are there any Japs among them? Soldiers, I mean."

"I can't say for sure, but there may be some. We've had some trouble with Japs coming out of the hills and stealing rations. They could probably mix with the Okinawans if they wanted to."

"Where'd you learn all this about the gooks?"

"Partly at a civil affairs school and partly from an old Okinawan who spent a few years in Hawaii. He remembers just enough English to be helpful and I've been using him as sort of straw boss. His name's Kaneshiro. I'll have him sent in to you in the morning if you want to talk to him. He's not a bad sort and you might find him useful."

"I think I can run this show without any help from a gook."

"Have it your own way. I don't know how you're going to communicate with them, though. None of your men speak Japanese, do they?"

"We're supposed to get an interpreter from Division, a doggie sergeant. He's a gook himself, but he was born in the States. Swenson's going to pick him up when he goes for rations tomorrow."

The doctor's cup was getting low and he refilled it and offered Rossi another drink.

"What's the scoop on this military government team of

yours?" Rossi asked. "They told me when they sent me up here that we'd be relieved within a week. As far as I'm concerned, the sooner the better."

"You probably know more about them than I do. I haven't heard from them since I came ashore. I imagine they're still lying off shore on the LST, if it hasn't actually turned around and gone back to Pearl. I thought I was coming ashore to look over a small group of civilians, a couple of dozen maybe. All I brought with me was my medical kit and a change of socks in case my feet got wet. A lieutenant picked up Loomis and me on the beach and brought us down here. There were two thousand refugees then and we never got away. After we'd been down here a couple of days another lieutenant showed up and said that we'd been transferred to Division on verbal orders. He said he'd try to get our gear down here but I haven't seen hide nor hair of him since."

"Didn't you ever try to get back to the beach and contact your outfit?"

"The gooks were coming in all day long and I never had a chance. I tried to get up to the beach one night but some idiot down the road started shooting at me."

"You were lucky he didn't open up with a machine gun."

"I thought there'd be a password or something."

"There is, but a lot of these characters are sort of trigger-happy."

"I guess I sound pretty green to you."

"You are. Look, doctor, why don't you ride up to Division with Swenson tomorrow. Somebody there can probably get you back to your outfit."

The doctor dabbed at some liquid that had trickled onto his chin. "I'd rather not."

"Don't tell me you like it here!"

"No."

Rossi looked at him sharply. "Don't get any ideas about being noble. You military government people all think you're sent out here to save suffering humanity. I'm running a stockade, not a Salvation Army mission. It won't make a damn bit of difference to me if a few gooks die because we don't have a doctor."

"I'll stay if you don't mind. If I go back now, it'll just mean coming back here again after a few days."

Rossi shrugged. "I thought you were pissed off at being sent down here."

"I was, but now that I'm here, I'd just as soon stay."

They drank in silence for a while. The doctor drank greedily but Rossi merely sipped at his drink as he lay on his back on the cot. At last the doctor settled down on the quilt and closed his eyes.

"Lord, I'm bushed," he said.

Rossi got up and went to the window. The trees were bending in a fresh breeze that smelled of rain. A candle was burning in Swenson's hut and Rossi could see Taliaferro stretched out on a cot, an arm thrown across his face.

"You know, Lieutenant," the doctor said, not opening his eyes, "I'm damn glad you showed up." Rossi said nothing and in a moment the doctor rolled over on his side and began to snore.

Rossi was still at the window when there was a crackling in the brush by the road as someone missed the path in the darkness. Rossi reached for his carbine.

"Who's there?"

The crackling stopped.

"Swenson."

"Come ahead."

Swenson came forward into the light from the window.

"You damn near got a hole through your head," Rossi said as he hung his carbine on the wall.

Swenson grinned and came inside. The doctor turned his face to the wall and buried his head in the quilt.

"What the hell's the matter with him?"

"Too much jungle juice." Rossi held the bottle out to Swenson. "Try some yourself."

"Jesus Christ! It tastes even worse than it smells." But Swenson sat down on the edge of the cot and took another drink. "Had some trouble up at post three. A couple of gooks tried to get past Davis."

"What happened?"

"They hung around for five, ten minutes. Davis finally kicked their asses back into the stockade. We ought to get some more wire, Lieutenant."

"What did they want?"

"Damned if I know. They came right up to Davis and made as if they wanted to get through. An old man and a kid."

"Why didn't he fire at them?"

"They sneaked up on him. He didn't know they were there until the kid was standing right in front of him."

"Davis can hear a can of beer being opened half a mile away; he can damn well hear a couple of gooks crashing around the mountainside."

"The men are sort of relaxed, Lieutenant. These gooks don't look as if they're going to make trouble."

"He must have thought it was a woman."

Swenson grinned.

"Tell Davis I want to see him first thing in the morning. You

24

can pass the word that after this you shoot first and find out who it is afterward."

"Suits me fine," Swenson said. He took a long pull at the bottle. "This stuff isn't bad once you get used to it."

"What do you make of this place?" Rossi asked.

"Hell, if I've got to mess around with gooks, I'd rather do it this way. I swear to God, Lieutenant, I'm getting goddamn sick and tired of taking chances on having my ass shot off by a gook."

"If it weren't so large it wouldn't make such a good target."

Swenson grinned delightedly. "Hell, Lieutenant, you can't drive a spike with a tack hammer."

"No screwing around," Rossi said.

"You know me, Lieutenant."

"That's what I mean. As far as I'm concerned, I'm not going to ask any questions if a gook or two just happens to get killed, but anyone I catch buddying up with them is going to wish he'd stayed down south. That includes gook women."

"Sure, Lieutenant." Swenson put down the bottle and helped Rossi carry the doctor to his room, where they left him fully dressed on his cot.

"You want to see Davis in the morning?"

"That's right."

"Okay, Lieutenant. Good night."

Swenson left but in a moment his face reappeared at the window.

"That crazy gee-sha's at it again."

Rossi stepped to the window. A thin, wild song was coming from the mountain.

"Sounds like a butchered hog," Swenson said. "Ever hear a hog get butchered?"

"No," Rossi said.

25

"Well," Swenson said after a while, "I guess I'll go hit the sack."

"Good night, Charley."

" 'Night, Lieutenant."

Four

OLD Kaneshiro sat on the doorsill of his hut and finished dressing. He carefully wrapped two worn and greasy strips of cotton around his withered shanks from his knees to the tops of his rubber-soled canvas shoes.

"I'm going out to take care of some business," he called into the house. His niece, blowsy in the early morning, came to the doorway, holding her dress about her with one hand, and gave Kaneshiro his hat, an antique gray felt with a conical crown. The old man crammed the hat down around his ears and adjusted the brim so that it would shade his eyes from the glare of the sun.

"Stay near the house," he warned his niece sharply. "The soldiers may come around today." The girl assented sleepily, combing her hair back from her forehead with her fingers.

"Pay attention to me," Kaneshiro ordered, and the girl shook herself to clear away her drowsiness. "Stay away from Shirayuki. I saw you talking to her at the well yesterday."

"Now, Uncle," the girl protested, "we were just passing the time of day."

"Listen to me!" Kaneshiro barked. "I said, stay away from her."

The girl nodded and Kaneshiro thrust his long, brass-bowled

27

pipe through his belt and set off. The girl remained in the doorway and watched him start down the path. He walked erectly in spite of his age and the impression he gave of military bearing was increased by the uniform he wore. His jacket, a garment of greenish khaki with a high collar and a row of flat, brassy buttons, had been salvaged from the barracks that had housed the Sugar Company's bespectacled young administrators. His pants, although they were only blue, workmen's trousers, were tucked into the makeshift puttees to give a semblance of riding breeches. As he turned out of the courtyard he broke off a short switch and slapped it smartly against his thigh. Even on the narrow, secluded trail behind the huts he walked stiffly, looking straight ahead and beating time with the switch as if he were marking cadence for a column of marching men.

The path led past the broken-down well where Swenson had stopped and on into a tangle of brush. A goat leaped nimbly out of his way as Kaneshiro struck at it ineffectually with his switch. He continued through the brush and came out in a gulley in the side of the mountain that was screened by trees from the main part of the stockade. A coil of thin smoke rose from a crude still where Gushiken, Kaneshiro's partner in this and other ventures, was blowing on a recalcitrant fire under a boiler. Gushiken crouched on the ground among his supplies: four straw sacks, only one of them full of rice, a wooden box of charcoal, a heap of sugar cane and two wide wooden tubs of mash. The air was sour with the penetrating ripeness of the mash.

Kaneshiro sat on the edge of the charcoal box and waited for Gushiken to finish with the fire. He dipped a finger into the mash and sniffed critically at the scum that clung to it.

"Not bad!" he called out. "A bit richer than last time."

Gushiken ignored him and continued to blow lustily on his fire. The charcoal flared up cherry-red under his breath but turned to a cold white ash when he paused to fill his lungs. The charcoal finally crackled steadily and Gushiken looked up and nodded morosely at Kaneshiro. His face was suffused with blood and when he spoke his voice came out in harsh gasps.

"The charcoal got wet last night," he said. "The tarpaulin's falling to pieces. You'll have to get some more; I'm too old to go through this performance every morning."

"We'll have to do something about it," Kaneshiro agreed calmly. "Your face looks like you'd been standing on your head for an hour."

"I have," Gushiken said, wiping his face with a cotton towel. When he was through, he twisted the towel lengthwise and tied it around his forehead, knotting it behind one ear. He squatted beside Kaneshiro and swirled his fingers through the mash.

"Not a bad batch," he observed with pride.

"Richer than last time," Kaneshiro repeated. He took his pipe from his belt and tamped a pinch of finely shredded tobacco into the bowl. Gushiken took an inch-long cigarette butt from behind his ear. Both men smoked without speaking for a few minutes. They heard in the distance the sounds of the stockade but in their gulley the only distraction was a muted rumbling that came from the boiler.

"The next batch will be the last," Gushiken said. "We're running out of both rice and cane."

"I'll take care of it," Kaneshiro said. "Don't worry about it."

"That's not all you're going to have to take care of. The joint between the tube and the boiler is coming loose. We ought to overhaul the whole machine. Instead of paying attention to the distilling I spend half my time patching up the holes in this broken-down contraption."

The boiler of the still was a large iron rice kettle, rifled from an unfortunate family of Koreans by Kaneshiro's grandson, an accomplished youngster who performed various services requiring stealth and agility. A wide tin funnel, rescued from the remains of a village store, was inverted over the mouth of the kettle. The spout of the funnel was cracked and had been patched with a strip of bark tied on with rusty wire where it joined the copper tube that led into a wooden bucket filled with water. The tube emerged from a well-caulked hole in the bottom of the bucket and discharged into a narrow-necked jar of glazed earthenware.

"It won't last much longer," Kaneshiro agreed.

A puff of steam escaped from the still and then a drop of clear yellow liquid formed on the mouth of the tube and hung trembling for a moment before dropping into the jar. Then there was another drop, and then another, and then more in rapid succession, until they joined in a thin, uninterrupted stream.

"Well," Gushiken said, "it may hold up after all until we get this batch done." He watched the operation of his still with quiet satisfaction. "Ah, it's going to behave itself this morning."

But in a moment there was a spurt of steam from the defective joint where the tube joined the funnel. Gushiken leaped to his feet and snatched the towel from his head to shield his hands from the steam. He finally subdued the leak and came away blowing on his fingers, which were red and tender in spite of the towel and their natural horniness.

"It's no good," he growled, "it won't do at all. That'll happen every five minutes from now on." He swung his hand through the air to cool it.

30

"It can't be helped," Kaneshiro said. "We'll have to make it do for now."

"It's all very well for you," Gushiken muttered rebelliously. "You get the rice and cane and take care of selling the stuff, but I'm the one who burns his fingers. 'Well, well,' you say. 'That's too bad.' 'It can't be helped.' 'We'll have to make it do for now.'" He fanned the air angrily with his injured hand, coming dangerously close to Kaneshiro's head.

"Now, now," Kaneshiro said soothingly. He fumbled in his pocket and brought forth a cigarette. It was a virgin cigarette, plump with tobacco, and wrapped in clean white paper. Gushiken automatically put it between his lips and Kaneshiro lighted a match and held it for him, but before the cigarette was lit, Gushiken tore it from his mouth and threw it to the ground.

"I'm tired," he shouted, "of trying to make fire with damp charcoal. I'm tired of burning my fingers in live steam. Most of all I'm tired of being bought off with these cheap cigarettes that have been mildewing in a damp cave for so long that they aren't even fit to keep the mosquitoes away." He stamped away angrily, avoiding Kaneshiro's eyes but watching the still cautiously.

Kaneshiro put his hand in his pocket again and this time he pulled out a whole pack. "Have another," he offered amiably.

Gushiken's brief revolt ended suddenly. He approached Kaneshiro shamefacedly, eyeing the pack of cigarettes intently. "Eh, it was an American cigarette." He stooped down to retrieve the cigarette he had refused but Kaneshiro stopped him. "No, no. Have a fresh one," Kaneshiro insisted. Gushiken lighted up and squatted on the ground, smoking peacefully.

Finally he chuckled. "Your grandson must have stolen it from a guard. A clever boy."

31

"As a matter of fact, it was given to me by my friend the sergeant," Kaneshiro said with dignity.

Gushiken slapped his thigh to show his appreciation of the enormity of the joke. "Your friend the sergeant!" he roared. "Hah!"

Kaneshiro waited until his friend's amusement had subsided. "It seems that the sergeant is a drinking man."

Gushiken looked at him warily, afraid either that the joke was being carried too far or that he had been lured into premature laughter. "I don't think we'll have any trouble over the rice and cane," Kaneshiro went on. "As a matter of fact, when you made a fool of yourself, I was about to tell you that I think we'll have to build a new still, probably bigger than this one. We might even have to make two."

Gushiken was at last convinced. "Well," he breathed in simple admiration, "well, well."

Kaneshiro got to his feet and smoothed the wrinkles out of his jacket. "To work!"

There was a hissing noise from the still and Gushiken leaped to the emergency. He damped a jet of steam with his towel and strained over the faulty connection. He screamed curses as he worked and howled with pain when a fresh blast stung his hand, but there was a new note of enthusiasm in his voice.

Kaneshiro returned along the path, passing his own dwelling, where his niece was sweeping out the courtyard, and then the jackstraw hovels where a colony of Koreans lived in a self-imposed ghetto. The unkempt women, more slatternly than the poorest of the Okinawans, glanced at Kaneshiro indifferently and went on with their unending household tasks, vainly attempting to bring order out of a chaos of dirty cooking utensils, unwashed laundry and snotty-nosed children. Kaneshiro strode

32

by them haughtily, beating time against his breeches with his switch until he came out on the open square.

The usual shrill cluster of women, carrying wooden buckets and battered tin cans were drawing water at the well. Carpenters were working on the new galley shed, nailing scraps of corrugated iron over a framework of rough-hewn lumber. Near the galley children played at making little cakes from the mud that had formed where a careless woman had spilled the water she was carrying home. A few lean and restless dogs roamed among the children, snapping voraciously at the mud tidbits they were offered. In the shade of the trees three shameless old men squatted companionably over a freshly dug slit trench.

Kaneshiro continued around the perimeter of the square until he came to where his friend the one-armed Taira was smoking his morning pipe. Taira was notoriously uncommunicative and Kaneshiro showed his respect for his friend's temperament by joining him without the formality of a greeting. The two old Okinawans watched the movement in the square. Two marines, both carrying rifles, were stationed at the road, guarding the women at the well and the children and the three shameless old men. Kaneshiro watched how the marines' heads would follow the women as they left the well and hurried toward their houses with their buckets of water.

"The sergeant," Taira said suddenly, pointing across the square with the stump of his arm. Swenson and a working party of Okinawans had come into sight, laden with tools and dragging a roll of barbed wire after them. They tore up the single strand of wire that the doctor had strung on unsteady posts between the stockade and the road and set about replacing it with a line of study posts sunk deep into the ground and carrying four strands of sharp-toothed wire. Swenson directed the

33

working party with gestures of his club which he accompanied with a profane litany. His crew worked steadily and soon a line of posts stretched along the road.

"A good soldier," Kaneshiro said in a professional tone. "He knows how to make men work."

"But he has a stupid face," Taira observed. "He eats too much — he looks like a pig."

"A good soldier," Kaneshiro repeated.

Taira watched a bright strand of wire creep across the front of the square from post to post. "Different from the old days."

Kaneshiro nodded agreement. In the old days the field workers had lived in the village that was now the center of the stockade. Neat paths had run from the square to the rows of two-family huts where the women did their laundry in the shade of the twisted pines. In the cool of the evening the men would squat in the open doorways, feeling the breeze on their faces while they sipped a weak, sour beer put up in unlabeled bottles by the Sugar Company. It was not a very good life, but neither was it a very bad one until, as the war went on, more and more of their wages were withheld, the prices at the company store crept upward, and special subscriptions were exacted for comfort kits for the soldiers in China.

The island's garrison, hard-bitten troops who had trained in skirmishes against the Russians on the Manchurian border, lived in barracks by the airstrip and when they passed through the cane workers' villages they barked out orders in the clipped accents of the home islands. The able-bodied villagers were drafted into a Home Defense Corps, but they had no rifles and drilled halfheartedly with fire-hardened bamboo spears. Kaneshiro, as befitted a man with the civilian rank of foreman, was made a sergeant and detailed to assist the unit's adjutant, a nerv-

34

ous bookkeeper from the Sugar Company's accounting office. For a memorable two days after the first enemy landing the Home Defense Corps, rechristened the Blood and Steel Special Attack Unit, had been in military control of the village and its environs. Then came the great backwash of the regular Japanese troops. After a brief and contemptuous inspection of the Special Attack Unit drawn up in parade formation, the major who commanded the infantry battalion that had bivouacked in the village suggested a number of imaginative but highly inappropriate uses for the unit's weapons.

The Special Attack Unit left the village indignantly but in good order that same night, charged with protecting civilians in an evacuation to a village in the south of the island. The evacuation was disrupted early the next morning by two strafing F-4U's and the unit never reassembled. Kaneshiro, abruptly abandoning his military career, had gathered together the remnants of his family: a niece, a grandson, and his brother's mother-in-law, and struck out for himself.

"Like pigs in a barnyard," Taira muttered, pointing with his stump to where the fourth and last strand of wire was being stretched along the posts. There was a gap between the two center posts for a gate, which was being constructed by two carpenters, working on the ground with saw and hammer. The men who had been working on the fence took a break, squatting on the ground around the carpenters. After they had rested for a few minutes, Swenson motioned them on and they disappeared behind the trees on the other side of the square.

"Things are going to change," Taira said. "Locked up like pigs."

"There are going to be some changes made," Kaneshiro

agreed, nodding sententiously. "It can't be helped. But, as long as they feed us — "

Taira snorted disdainfully.

"All in all, it's better than it was down south," Kaneshiro pointed out.

"Perhaps so. Perhaps not."

After the dispersion of the Special Attack Unit, Kaneshiro had led his family to a cave in the rocky cliffs along the coast, south of the escarpment where the Japanese were digging in for the last great counterattack that was to sweep the enemy from the island. Other refugees had joined them in the cave until half a dozen families had crowded into the clammy darkness. At first Kaneshiro had begged rations from a nearby battery of artillery but on the third day he had been driven away at the point of a bayonet. Kaneshiro and his grandson foraged farther afield but their diet grew slimmer and within the week two infants wasted away when their mothers' breasts went dry. Only the fat black rats that scuttled over the floor of the cave, as soon as the sun had set, seemed to find nourishment.

On the tenth day visitors had come to the cave, a lieutenant accompanied by a squad of soldiers. The lieutenant made no effort to conceal his loathing as he flashed his light into the dark corners of the cave where the refugees cowered among their bundles of bedding. Kaneshiro attempted to ingratiate himself with the officer, but the lieutenant brushed him off curtly. He was a thin-faced, ascetic-looking man, elegant in spite of his muddy uniform, and when he spoke it was with a precise, scholarly inflection.

"The time has come," he told the refugees, "for us to perform our final duty to the Emperor. The defenders of the escarpment

36

will fight to the last, but that will be very soon. In short, there is no more ammunition and no more food. When the enemy comes, he will find only death and destruction." He beckoned with his flashlight. "Come!"

"But the counterattack," Kaneshiro protested. "The reinforcements from the Philippines — "

"There will be no reinforcements," the lieutenant said coldly. He walked out without looking back but his men remained at the mouth of the cave with their rifles at the ready, and so the refugees, Kaneshiro among them, filed out quietly and followed the lieutenant into the hollow below the cave. Only Kaneshiro's brother's mother-in-law, old and crippled, was overlooked where she lay in the darkest shadow of the cave.

They had gone fifty yards or so before Kaneshiro realized that he did not want to die. Their path was a rocky trail, and Kaneshiro, suddenly gone clumsy, stumbled repeatedly until, flanked by his grandson and his niece, he had fallen well to the rear of the little procession. The attention of the soldier bringing up the rear, a stupid-faced boy of eighteen, was diverted by a burst of firing from not far away. Kaneshiro slipped behind a clump of rocks and brush, dragging the children with him. Their escape went undetected and from their observation post they watched the remainder of the party descend into the hollow.

The soldiers herded the Okinawans around the single pine tree that spread its knotty roots over the rocky ground of the hollow. The Okinawans clustered together obediently and made no attempt to interfere as the soldiers moved among them to go about their business. They watched as a satchel charge was rigged up at the foot of the tree and yet they remained where they were when the soldiers retreated to a safe distance. A little girl, strapped too tightly to her mother's back, wailed with pain and hunger but otherwise the little band was silent. Two or three of them lifted their heads and looked toward the cave, as if regretting some forgotten possession, or out over the sea, where an enemy picket boat cruised in a leisurely, holiday fashion. A faint sputtering noise came from the fuse that was attached to the explosive.

"*Banzai!*" cried the lieutenant.

The refugees responded weakly.

"*Banzai!*" the lieutenant cried again.

One of the Okinawans raised his arms above his head and shouted an answer.

"*Banzai!*" the lieutenant shouted for the last time. There was a sudden panic around the tree; the crowd scattered but they were too late.

Not all of the Okinawans were killed outright. The survivors struggled on the ground, shrieking with pain and fear. Those who could crawled away from the severed trunk of the tree. The lieutenant screamed an order and there was a volley of shots. More bodies twitched on the ground but the survivors continued to crawl toward the soldiers. When their ammunition was gone the soldiers beat them back with the butts of their rifles. It was over quickly.

While the soldiers stacked their rifles the lieutenant and a sergeant moved in among their victims and administered the final, merciful strokes with their swords. As if it were a military evolution in which they had been trained, the men knelt on the ground and, taking grenades from their pockets, held them against their bellies. When the last of the grenades had exploded, the conscientious sergeant, having assured himself that none of his men was shamming, fell on his sword. The lieutenant, alone at last in the hollow, took his pistol from his holster and put a bullet through his head.

It was only then that Kaneshiro and the two terrified children returned to the cave, where the girl's grandmother was whining in a dark recess. They had stayed there — Kaneshiro, the old woman, the young girl, and the boy — until a patrol of marines discovered their sanctuary.

The marines sent them back to a collecting point where they joined hundreds of other refugees who had also been driven out of their hiding places in the caves that honeycombed the shoreline. After a long day's wait in the relentless sun they were formed into columns and began the slow march toward the mountains. The columns crawled painfully along the dusty road where they completely snarled up the southbound ammunition and ration trucks. A score of the sick and wounded died along the route of march. The old and the weak soon fell out along the side of the road. Kaneshiro abandoned his brother's mother-in-law in a canefield where, with other old crones, she squatted and watched the dusty column with beady eyes, grumbling querulously at the orphaned children who whimpered among the green stalks of sugar cane. Somebody ordered the trucks to pick up the old women and the children on the return trip, and they, too, were carried north toward the mountain.

"And now the lieutenant," Taira said.

Rossi had appeared by the gate, where he was conferring with Swenson. He and Swenson watched the carpenters, who were nearing the end of their work. They raised the gate they had fashioned from heavy, unfinished logs and fitted it between the gateposts and drove in the long spikes that secured the hinges. Finally they closed the gate and lifted a thick wooden bar that fitted across the posts. It dropped into place with a thud that was heard clearly across the square.

"You see: like pigs in a barnyard," Taira said.

Kaneshiro nodded. "I have to go. Have you seen Shirayuki?"

Taira leered at him. "Eh, making arrangements for your niece?"

"No," Kaneshiro said stiffly. "What do you mean?"

Taira heaved with sudden, bawdy laughter. "A nice piece, your niece. She ought to bring a good price."

Kaneshiro spat on the ground at Taira's feet. "You horny old fool!"

Taira went on laughing, his weathered face knotted with merriment. Kaneshiro got to his feet and started back toward his hut.

"Not that way!" Taira called after him. "An hour ago I saw her with Tanaka, the girl with the bad arm. Try the hospital." Kaneshiro grunted his thanks and changed his course.

As he crossed the square he was stopped by three of the women who had been at the well. A family had been passed over in the distribution of the rice ration. Another was billeted in a hut without a roof. A quilt had been stolen — probably by the Koreans. "Afterwards, afterwards," Kaneshiro told them all, tempering the brusqueness of his reply with a politic smile.

Sick bay was located in the largest and least damaged building in the stockade. There was a ward for the bed cases, a dressing room with a crude operating table, and a kitchen. It was the hour of morning sick call and the ambulatory patients formed a line that straggled far down the path. The wooden screens that formed the walls of the building had been removed for the day and the patients in the ward lay on pallets on the floor, protected from the sun but open to a breeze that carried away the smells of sickness and death. They were packed together so tightly that there was barely enough room for the squinty-eyed girl who acted as nurse to crawl on her hands and knees between them, carrying water and food to the convalescent or inexpertly feeling the pulse of the dying.

The doctor and Loomis sat at a table on which were a few simple instruments, jars of medicine and rolls of gauze. Each of them was attending to a patient.

"What ho!" the doctor greeted Kaneshiro. "How's business?"

"No good," Kaneshiro answered sourly. "No damn good."

"What you need is a vacation. Why don't you take a week's leave and go back to Hilo? Lie in the sun all day, drink okolehao all night, maybe get yourself a little wahine to do the cooking and make your bed."

"Sure, Doc. I think I go tomorrow."

They both laughed immoderately, indulgent of their foolishness. It was their standard pleasantry. Loomis did not join in. He continued to work, cutting off the old dressings, cleaning out the wounds, applying new dressings. The line of patients at his side of the table moved faster than the line at the doctor's, and there was no laughter. The doctor was continually diverted by attempts to communicate with his patients in pidgin Japanese. Kaneshiro sat down at the entrance to the dressing room and lighted his pipe.

Shirayuki and the girl Tanaka were waiting their turn in Loomis's line. Shirayuki was a handsome, well-built woman dressed in a blue shirt and baggy, blue farmer-woman's trousers. Her black hair was drawn back from her forehead and coiled in a glossy knot at the nape of her neck. She chatted with the other patients in a low, husky voice. The girl with her was a wispy creature, wearing a patched dress of purple rayon. Her abundant hair framed a sharp, pinched face, like that of a frightened mouse. Above the elbow, one arm was wrapped in a dirty dressing. Neither she nor Shirayuki acknowledged Kaneshiro's presence. He puffed patiently at his pipe, exchanging greetings with the other patients and occasionally helping the doctor out with a word of Japanese.

Presently Shirayuki and the girl were abreast of Loomis. Loomis clipped the dressing from the girl's arm and laid bare an ugly gash. While he was picking lint from the wound with a pair of tweezers the girl yelped with sudden pain.

"Lay off that girl," the doctor warned him sharply. "That's the second time that's happened today."

"My hand slipped," Loomis said, watching a drop of blood oozing from the girl's arm.

"You're too good a corpsman for that sort of an excuse," the doctor said. "You just don't make mistakes, Loomis."

Loomis went on with his work without acknowledging the doctor's rebuke. When he was through, Shirayuki took the girl by the hand and led her to the doctor.

"Sankyou," the girl whispered.

"You're welcome. If I were twenty years younger I might take out my fee in trade. Run along now and don't get into any trouble."

Kaneshiro arose from his seat by the doctor and followed the two women, catching up with them when they were out of sight of sick bay.

"Shirayuki-san," he said. "I have some important business to discuss with you."

Shirayuki sent the girl on ahead and waited, impassive and faintly hostile, for Kaneshiro to begin.

42

Five

TWO trucks carrying new prisoners pulled up at the gate where Fischer stood guard. The wiry colored boy who drove the first truck leaped from the cab and let down the tail gate, but Fischer, armed and truculent, prevented him from unloading the prisoners.

"You ain't going to dump no gooks here without the sergeant knowing. I'm going to shoot the first gook that gets off of that truck."

The driver leaned against the side of his truck and regarded Fischer bleakly. "I'm not moving this truck until the gooks are all unloaded." He was joined by the driver of the second truck, a burly, white pfc with tattooed arms. Fischer retreated toward the gate, keeping both drivers covered with his weapon.

"I guess you guys aren't in any hurry. I just remembered the sergeant's gone up to Division."

The tattooed driver shrugged and turned back to his own truck. "You better find him or someone else in about two minutes. I'm pulling out of here and I'm not taking any of these gooks with me."

Fischer swung the muzzle of his rifle from one driver to the other. "Go ahead," he said.

Rossi working in his hut, heard the sounds of argument and

hurried to the gate to forestall one of the incidents that frequently developed when Fischer was left at the mercy of his own obstinacy.

The prisoners on the platforms of the trucks were packed together so tightly that those by the tail gate were in constant danger of tumbling to the ground. Fischer eyed them menacingly as they fought to keep clear of the edge of the platform.

"Now what the hell's going on?" Rossi demanded.

The tattooed driver spoke up. "Damned if I know, Lieutenant. This crazy bastard seems to be figuring on shooting us."

"I told these guys they couldn't go dumping gooks anywhere they wanted to."

"Ah, relax, Fischer," Rossi said. "And for Christ's sake put that rifle down. Now, where'd these gooks come from?"

"Well, we were coming back from a run to the new airstrip when a major stopped us and loaded them on. Said they'd been hanging around his battalion for two days and he was going to go bats if he had to put up with them for another day. He got sort of chickenshit about it so we brought them along."

"Who told you to bring them here? This stockade's so full of gooks now that I can't take care of them all."

The tattooed driver shook his head in sympathy. "You got your troubles, Lieutenant, and I got mine. This truck was due back an hour ago. I don't know where these gooks are supposed to go, but they're getting out of my truck right here."

"I guess I can't stop you," Rossi said. "Go ahead and unload them."

The prisoners were persuaded by the driver to crawl off the end of the platform. They came slowly and carefully, as if they were afraid to trust their emaciated bodies to the short jump to the ground. At last there were only two small boys and an

44

old woman left in the first truck. The boys cowered against the back of the cab and the old woman lay on the platform with her eyes closed, indifferent to the commotion around her. The driver jumped onto the platform and handed the boys to Rossi, who deposited them, sniffling and wailing, on the ground. The old woman was swung down like a sack of meal.

The new prisoners were a highly unprepossessing lot — thin, dirty, and dressed in rags. A group of Okinawans, among them Kaneshiro's niece, had gathered inside the wire and were looking on curiously, but without any evident sympathy. The tattooed driver spotted Kaneshiro's niece.

"Say, Lieutenant, you got many more like her?"

"We got a million of them. What's it to you?"

"Well, maybe I could change my mind about staying down here a while longer. For a gook, that little girl ain't bad at all. I can't say that I mind a little piece of dark meat now and then." The colored driver looked studiously away.

"You better get in that truck and get moving. You can pass the word to your friends that my men have orders to shoot at anyone they don't think has any business in the stockade."

The driver shrugged. "Have it your own way, Lieutenant."

Taliaferro appeared in time to see the last prisoners unloaded from the second truck. They had hardly reached the ground before the drivers slammed the tail gates up, put their trucks in gear, and swung off down the road.

"Get them in the stockade," Rossi said.

Fischer unbarred the gate and swung it wide. The Okinawans inside backed away slowly, begrudging the newcomers a few square feet of the stockade.

"Give them room," Taliaferro urged. "Come on now, get back there."

The new prisoners filed through the gate and gathered in a tight, unhappy group. Rossi and Taliaferro followed them into the stockade and Fischer closed and barred the gate behind them.

"See that these gooks get quartered somewhere. You'd better make sure that they get fed; most of them look as if they hadn't had a decent meal in a couple of months."

"Sure, Lieutenant," Taliaferro drawled and turned to the Okinawans. "Now look here, you gooks, you got to find some room for these new gooks." He pointed to the new prisoners and made a roof with his hands. "You got to see that they get something to eat." He went through the motions of eating from a bowl with chopsticks. "Get going now, chop-chop."

The prisoners received the pantomime in silence.

"Well, I've told them," Taliaferro said, "but they don't seem to get the idea. What do I do now, Lieutenant?"

"Keep trying," Rossi said. "They'll catch on."

Taliaferro repeated his performance, accompanying it with a more elaborate commentary. This time there was some movement in the rear ranks of the crowd. The movement worked toward the front and Kaneshiro was expelled into the space between the crowd and the new prisoners. He greeted Rossi with a gesture that might have been a military salute.

"I am Kaneshiro," he announced. "Live in Hilo three years. Got a nice place in Hilo, make lot of money, go to movies every week. Bette Davis, Joan Crawford, Deanna Durbin, Shirley Temple. Have big house, big family. Make lot of luau for friend, drink okolehao. But I get stupid and go back to Okinawa to see family, can't go back to Hilo." He struck himself across the forehead and shook his head dolefully.

"What do you want me to do for you?"

46

Kaneshiro spread his hands palms upward. "Nothing. I fix these goddamn gooks for you, eh?"

"What's your angle?" Rossi demanded. "What do you think you're going to get out of this?"

Kaneshiro let his hands fall to his sides. It was evident that in a moment he would turn away rebuffed, his generous offer misconstrued.

"All right, you fix them up. See that they get some chow. If you need to make some shelters, see the guard and he'll get you some canvas. Take this old woman and any others that need it up to sick bay. I want things squared away by sundown. Do you understand?"

"Sure," Kaneshiro said, "okay." He faced the crowd behind the new prisoners. *"Minna-san, Chui-dono ga —"*

Rossi and Taliaferro remained in the stockade until Kaneshiro was through with his speech. The crowd broke up into small parties that began to carry out Kaneshiro's instructions.

"You want me to stick around?" Taliaferro asked.

"You better get back to the fence detail, Tolly. The gook seems to know what he's doing. Fischer can keep an eye on them."

Kaneshiro saw them through the gate with another of his flamboyant salutes.

When Swenson came back from Division, he brought with him a new man, wearing dungarees of a different shade and cut than the marines'. His ankle-high boots gleamed with a rich luster when he got out of the jeep. He was wearing a khaki overseas cap, pressed until its creases were knife edges; sewed on the cap was the emblem of a white parachute on a blue circle. Paratrooper's wings had been inked onto his jacket above the left pocket. The paratrooper himself was small and brown and his features were formed in the same mold as those of the prisoners in the stockade. Rossi waited outside his hut for Swenson and the new man to approach.

"What luck, Charley?" Rossi called to Swenson, ignoring his companion.

"I got the rations. They didn't have any Chesterfields so I brought you a carton of Old Golds. This is the doggie that talks Japanese."

Rossi turned his attention to the soldier, who was standing at ease. "What the hell have you done to your carbine, Sergeant?" The carbine that was slung over his shoulder appeared to have been sawed off just below the pistol grip. He took the carbine from his shoulder and snapped into place a stock made of heavy wire that had been folded back against the rest of the weapon.

"Paratroop issue, sir."

Rossi took the carbine from him and weighed it in his hands. He snapped the stock back and forth and then handed the weapon to Swenson. "My God, Charley, the army's getting fancy-pants these days."

Swenson grinned and tested the action of the wire stock before handing the carbine back to its owner.

"So you're a paratrooper," Rossi said. "What are you doing here?"

"I wish I knew, Lieutenant. When they shipped me out I thought I was going to make some jumps. I enlisted in the army because I wanted to kill Japs. Instead I end up translating diaries for an officer at D-2."

"What's your name?"

"Mike Murayama."

"Are you Japanese?"

48

"I was born in Oregon, Lieutenant."

"Your folks were Japanese."

"That's right, sir."

"I don't like Japs and I didn't ask for you to be sent here, but now that you're here I guess I'll have to put you to work."

"I didn't ask to come, Lieutenant."

Rossi grunted and inspected Mike from head to toe.

"I don't like those goddamn paratroop boots. While you're here you can wear boondockers like the rest of us."

Mike didn't answer.

"Furthermore, you can stow away that fancy pisscutter and wear a helmet while you're on duty. You have a helmet, don't you?"

"Yes, sir."

"Did you leave your gear in the jeep?"

Mike nodded.

"You can pick it up later. Charley, take this man up to sick bay. The doctor can probably use him. We got a new batch of gooks in this afternoon."

Swenson and Mike started toward the stockade. "Come back here," Rossi ordered. "I just want to make one thing plain, Sergeant. I've told my men that I'm going to make it rough for any of them I catch buddying up to the gooks. See that you don't use your Japanese off duty. If you behave yourself, we'll get along; if you don't, I can make things pretty tough for you."

"I think I get the idea," Mike said. "I told you I came out here to fight Japs. Is there anything else, sir?"

"Just one more thing. In the army you may be a sergeant, but as far as this outfit's concerned, you're just a pfc. Do you follow me?"

"Yes, sir. I think I'm beginning to get the picture."

The doctor's face, tired and peevish, lighted up when he saw who was with Swenson.

"You must be the man who speaks Japanese."

"That's right," Mike said. He remained in the doorway of the dressing room, taking no chances on being rebuffed again.

"Come in, come in," the doctor invited. "I hope Lieutenant Rossi's going to let you help us out here."

"He's all yours, Doctor," Swenson said. "The lieutenant said to bring him up here and see if you could use him."

The doctor peered quizzically at Swenson. "That's very kind of Lieutenant Rossi," he said slowly. "Please convey my thanks to him. I'm delighted. But I don't understand why in hell he's being so generous."

Swenson grinned. "I'll tell him," he promised. "I got to shove off now. You come see me when the doctor's through with you, Junior. We'll see if we can't fix you up a sack somewhere."

Mike stood awkwardly in the entrance to the dressing room while the doctor, frowning, watched Swenson going down the path to the square. Behind them Loomis worked on the old woman who had been carried out of the truck.

"Rossi give you a bad time?"

"It could have been worse," Mike said. "But not much."

The doctor grunted and took Mike by the arm and drew him into the room. "Come on," he said, "I'm going to put you to work right away. As a matter of fact, I'm damn glad Rossi decided to assign you to me. If I can find out what's wrong with some of these people I may be able to do something for them. I've been working by God and by guess and by this little green book." He took a mimeographed manual, dog-eared and stained, from the operating table and showed it to Mike. "All I've learned from this is to say '*Doko ga itai des'ka*,' and as often as not they

50

don't even understand that." Mike smiled briefly, showing white, even teeth.

"This is Loomis, my corpsman," the doctor said. Loomis looked up and nodded and then went on tending the old woman.

"Incidentally, I don't know *your* name."

"Murayama. Mike Murayama."

"Michael Murayama. Catholic?"

"No, Buddhist. Mike's short for Masakichi."

The doctor laughed apologetically. "It's still a good name. What do you like to be called?"

"I answer to Mike."

Mike sniffed the air tentatively. There was a stringent antiseptic smell, and, less noticeable at first, the bitter oiliness of a disinfectant cleaning solution, but through both of these came another, a more human smell.

"It's the patients in the ward," the doctor said. "I'm afraid we can't bathe them every day. Come on over here, Mike, I have a job for you."

An old man and a boy, possibly his grandson, squatted on the floor beside the operating table. They both coughed frequently, in dry, hacking spasms, and a trickle of phlegm dribbled from a corner of the boy's mouth. The old man hawked and spat out a great semisolid gob of blood-flecked matter. The hacking in his chest shook his withered frame unmercifully. The boy was beyond crying; he remained dumb except for the recurrent fits of coughing, and when the doctor and Mike approached neither he nor the old man raised their eyes from the ground.

"These two cases came in only this afternoon. I can't figure out exactly what's the matter with them. If you can get them talking we might be able to do something for them."

51

Mike began to speak to the old man, at first in a matter-of-fact tone and then wheedlingly. He persisted and at last the old man looked up and answered him in a flat, rasping voice.

"He says he and the boy and the rest of their family were in a cave down below the escarpment. They had enough food and stuck it out for a long time after they knew the Japs had lost the island. One day what he calls a smoke bomb burst inside the cave. Only he and the boy got out. They were knocked out for a while and they've been coughing ever since. He says the men who captured them gave them some food but he couldn't hold it on his stomach. He wants to know if they're going to die."

"Smoke," the doctor said. "It sounds like phosphorous. That damned stuff burns the tissue right out of your lungs."

The boy began to whimper. He opened his mouth to cry and a stream of thick matter bubbled over his lips. The old man watched Mike and the doctor with dull, patient eyes.

Loomis turned from the old woman and inspected the doctor's patients. "They're goners, Doc. You're wasting your time."

The doctor was annoyed by Loomis's interruption. "It's never too late," he said. "We can always make it easier for them." He took a bottle from the rack on the table and spilled several white pills into the palm of his hand and gave them to Mike.

"Tell them to take one of these every hour. If they're not better tomorrow, come up and see me again. We don't have any room in the ward for them; ask Swenson if he can't find them a quiet place to stay."

Loomis lifted an eyebrow and smiled sidelong at the doctor. "Those are APC's, Doc. They won't do them any more good than a glass of root beer."

"I know it," the doctor said. "There's nothing I can do that'll help them. All I'm trying to do is to let them know that I'm doing everything I can. It might make it easier for them."

The old man had taken the pills from Mike and was holding them in his open hand, waiting for the doctor's instructions. He spoke again in his terrible rasping voice.

"He wants to know again if he's going to die. What'll I tell him?"

The doctor was silent and Loomis spoke up. "Tell them to go find a nice, comfortable place to die."

There was a long silence until the doctor got to his feet. "Oh, Christ! Tell them anything you want. I wasn't cut out for this sort of a job." He walked away stiffly, disappearing around the corner of the building.

Mike spoke, gently and at length, to the old man while Loomis watched curiously. When Mike was through, the old man nodded and fingered one of the pills thoughtfully. He smiled, a wretched but grateful smile, and pressed a pill into the boy's hand.

Loomis laughed. He took one of the pills from the old man and flipped it into the air and let it fall to the floor where it rolled into a crack between the boards. Loomis laughed again and shook his head. The old man turned to Mike but Mike looked away and said nothing. The old man let the rest of the pills fall to the floor and pulled the boy to his feet and led him away.

"Well, I guess we told them," Loomis observed.

Mike watched the two dying prisoners go down the path, the boy still clutching the APC tablet in his fist.

"You're a real cold-blooded son of a bitch, aren't you?"

"Yeah, that's what a lot of people think," Loomis said without rancor.

53

When he returned to the square, Mike was caught in the middle of a mass rush toward the galley. A great disorderly crowd of prisoners, each one fearing that he would be left waiting with an empty rice bowl, milled around the kettles. Mike shouted at them to clear a path and worked vigorously with his elbows, but he was carried in a great surge toward the kettles and didn't break entirely free until he was nearly at the gate. The marine who stood guard at the gate put down his rifle and unbarred the gate.

"Haven't seen anything like it since I left the farm," the marine observed.

Mike rubbed his side, sore from contact with a dozen elbows. "Does this go on every night?"

"This is the first meal they've cooked at the galley. I guess it's going to be like this from now on."

A shout came from back in the square. "Hey, Junior. Come over here."

"I guess the sergeant wants you," the marine said.

"I don't answer to Junior," Mike said. "If he wants me he can call me by my name."

Swenson raised his voice again. "Goddammit, Junior, when I call you, come on the double."

"Looks like your name's Junior," the marine said. "He's been calling me meathead for two years now. It burns my ass every time, but I answer to it. If I was you I'd get over there before he gets mad." He swung the gate to and barred it before Mike had indicated that he was going to follow his advice.

Swenson was hidden among the trees behind the galley. With him was a woman. She turned away from Swenson and smiled at Mike.

"You didn't break your ass getting over here," Swenson said.

"I don't answer to Junior," Mike said. "If you want me call me by my name."

"Sure," Swenson said, "sure. Find out what's eating this babe, Junior."

"Now look: You probably don't believe this but if I wanted to I could break you in half. The only reason I don't is because I know I don't have to put up with this crap."

"You're a cocky little bastard, aren't you?"

"I can take care of myself."

Swenson laughed suddenly. "By God, I bet you can."

The woman unfolded her story to Mike. He listened to her without interrupting and then translated for Swenson's benefit.

"She says she's done business in Japan, Manchuria, the Philippines, and finally here, and this stockade is the first place she's been where she's run into soldiers who don't know a piece of ass when they see it. She claims to have been the madame of the officers' cathouse. Some of her girls are still with her and she'd like to get back into business. She wants permission to speak to the lieutenant about it."

"The lieutenant would pop a gut. Tell her he wouldn't be interested."

"She says, why not?"

Swenson frowned. "I'm damned if I know. He just doesn't stand for that sort of stuff."

The Madame accepted this explanation with good-natured puzzlement. "How's she going to go into business if the lieutenant's against it?"

"Tell her I'll take care of that. Say, ask her if she knows a little dolly that lives with this old gook Kaneshiro. A pretty little girl, about eighteen years old."

Mike conferred briefly with the Madame. "She knows her."

55

"Tell her that if she'll fix things up for me with that little girl, I'll see that the lieutenant doesn't make any trouble for her."

"She still wants to know why she has to stay clear of the lieutenant. She says she likes his looks."

"Just tell her to stay away from him if she knows what's good for her. What does she say about that little girl?"

"She knows her, but this man Kaneshiro's already been kicking up a fuss. He doesn't like the idea of her making friends with his niece. Besides, he claims to be boss of the stockade and he thinks he ought to get a cut on any profits she makes. She wants to know if that's the straight poop."

"If Kaneshiro bothers her, tell her to come to me. That old gook's getting too many ideas of his own. We'll talk to her about it again."

The Madame thanked Mike gravely, bowed to Swenson, and left them. She carried herself well, walking gracefully with her head held proudly erect.

"Sometimes I wish I knew this gook language," Swenson said.

"It comes in handy," Mike agreed. They started toward the gate.

"You know," Swenson said, "it seems to me the lieutenant has the wrong angle on you. I think I'd better talk to him about it. I'd like to fix things so you can give me a hand with the gooks. The doctor isn't going to need you more than a couple of hours a day."

"It sounds okay to me. Just as long as I don't have to brown-nose. I'm not going to take any crap from that guy."

"The lieutenant's all right," Swenson said. "He's just got a peculiar way of looking at things."

Fischer let them through the gate and they walked toward the jeep to get Mike's gear.

"I've been thinking," Swenson said. "The barracks' pretty crowded. Taliaferro, he's a buddy of mine, and I got some room in our shack. Maybe you could move in with us."

"It's okay with me," Mike said.

"Sure. I don't know why I didn't think of it before."

Six

THE headmen Kaneshiro had chosen assembled in the square after breakfast, gathering at one side of the row of giant iron pots that were under the galley shed. Two men, an old woman, and a dozen children, stragglers who had missed breakfast, were scraping morsels of cold, caked rice from inside the pots. Kaneshiro ordered them away. The stragglers hesitated for a moment and then, full of resentment, compromised by moving to the kettle farthest from Kaneshiro's group. The other prisoners in the busy square gave the galley a wide berth.

The gate to the stockade clattered shut and Swenson and Mike approached the headmen. Swenson, as usual, was carrying his club, which he flourished in emphatic gestures to punctuate his discourse to Mike, who nodded absently, still sleepy. Kaneshiro jammed his conical hat firmly on his head and joined them. He was followed by his grandson, whom Swenson recognized as the leader of the group of boys he had caught tormenting a puppy. The boy grinned at him and Swenson swung playfully at him with his club.

Swenson inspected the headmen, who stared back at him with rheumy eyes. "What the hell is this? The Oldest Inhabitants Club?"

Kaneshiro laughed uncertainly. "Old men," he said.

The old men waited, silent and solemn, for Swenson to give hem the word.

"All right, now get this. Each one of you's personally responsible for his own people."

Mike interpreted.

"Pass the word that there's to be no cooking in quarters. Everybody lines up here at chow time. And I don't want to see any more trouble like there was last night."

The grim old men gave no sign that they had understood.

"Nobody goes near the wire. Nobody messes around with he guards. Nobody goes up to sick bay unless they have business there."

Mike interpreted again.

"I don't give a damn how you manage things in your own groups, but don't bother me. The first time there's trouble in any of your groups, the whole group goes without chow for he day. The second time, one of you is going to get locked up in the cage on the hill."

"You sure they got that about being locked up with the nuts?" Swenson asked Mike. Mike repeated the warning. This time the old men nodded solemnly when he had finished.

"That's all," Swenson said. "Break it up now. Kaneshiro, you old bastard, get me a working party to go after the rice."

The headmen departed without breaking their judicious silence. Kaneshiro scurried about among the people in the square. He returned leading a squad of sturdy women.

"Don't the men do any work around this place?"

"It's okay," Mike said. "In Okinawa the women do the carrying. They're used to it. One of those women can probably lift twice as much as you can."

59

Kaneshiro wrinkled up his old face and winked significantly. "How about whisky rice?"

"Plenty of whisky rice," Swenson said. "Mike, see that the old gook gets an extra sack for himself."

Mike led Kaneshiro and the women through the gate, where they picked up Davis, who followed the procession up the road toward the old warehouse, cradling a BAR in his arms.

Fischer, who was on guard again, detained Swenson at the gate.

"Say, Charley, I hear you're cooking up something."

"Yeah?" Swenson said cautiously. "Where'd you hear that?"

"Just scuttlebutt. Some of the boys were talking last night."

"You guys talk too much. If you didn't talk so much, Meathead, you might make corporal some day."

"All I was going to say was that if you were organizing anything, I'd like a piece. Just a little piece."

"You know damn well the lieutenant would blow a gasket if he thought anything funny was going on," Swenson said righteously. "Christ! You think I want to stand guard with the rest of you yardbirds?"

"I was just going to say that it wouldn't look good if you kept it all for you and Taliaferro and that doggie that's moved in with you."

"The boys been talking about that too?"

"Yeah. It looks funny, this doggie moving right in and taking over."

"He's not taking over anything," Swenson said. "He's a good joe."

"I didn't say he wasn't. Just the same, I don't think the boys are going to like it if you keep it all to yourselves. There's plenty to go around."

Swenson considered this with an air of judicial contemplation. "You keep your nose clean, Meathead, and maybe I'll save you a piece. A little bitty piece. You can tell the boys that what the lieutenant says, goes. If I catch any of them messing around on their own, they're really going to find their asses in a sling."

"Sure," Fischer said. "I just thought I'd say something about it."

Swenson crossed the road and went toward Rossi's hut.

The round concrete top of the cistern behind the hut was warm from the afternoon sun, still high above the trees. Rossi stood on the edge of the concrete slab and, lifting a bucket of water high over his head, sluiced down his naked body with cold water that had a faint metallic smell. He shivered slightly as the water coursed down his body and trickled over the side of the cistern and onto the ground. He began to soap himself down, starting with his hair and working the thin suds over his neck and shoulders.

Swenson sat in the window in the back of the hut with his legs hanging outside. "Taliaferro found a dead cat in our cistern," he said conversationally.

"Get it out?"

"Yeah, but that meathead Fischer fell in when he went after it."

"Hurt himself?"

"Nah," Swenson said with disgust. "Fischer has a head like a rock. But the water still smells funny. We don't know if it's the cat or Fischer."

Rossi drew another bucket of water and washed off the soap that was beginning to dry on the upper half of his body.

"You still got some soap in your hair," Swenson said.

61

Rossi poured the rest of the water over his head.

"You got it that time."

Rossi began to work the soap along his legs.

"The stockade's shaping up pretty good," Swenson said. "I think we got the gooks organized okay."

"It's about time. What the hell was going on at the galley last night? It looked like somebody started a riot."

"The gooks got out of hand at chow call. I'll get that business squared away today."

"How's that doggie sergeant making out? I notice he's bunking with you."

"Well, I took him up to sick bay like you told me, but the doctor can't use him more than a couple of hours a day. He's been helping me in the stockade. He's not a bad guy, Lieutenant, and he really knows how to give the gooks the word."

"I guess I was sort of rough on him," Rossi said. "I still don't trust that son of a bitch, but I guess we can use him all right." Rossi took his towel and began to dry himself. "How're the rest of the men doing?"

"They seem to like it all right. Plenty of sack time and the chow's not too bad. I fixed it so the gook women are going to do our laundry. I'll send a man over to pick up anything you want done."

"About the women: I noticed Fischer trailing a little gook girl around the stockade like a hound dog after a bitch in heat."

"That asshound Fischer won't make any trouble," Swenson said contemptuously. "He's not smart enough to really get in trouble."

"He's not the only one I've seen talking to gook women. Who was that lady friend of yours last night?"

"That's probably the woman who's taking care of the laundry," Swenson said glibly.

"I'll bet it was," Rossi said. "Not a bad-looking woman."

Swenson let it pass. "I was thinking, Lieutenant, now we got the place organized, maybe it would be a good idea if we let the gooks do some of the work. I can't keep an eye on everything that goes on."

Rossi said nothing and went on scrubbing with his towel at the grime that still clung to his ankles.

"You know this old gook that lived in Hawaii? He seems to know what the score is so I've been letting him take care of some things I can't be bothered with. One thing I want him to do is to get this chow situation straightened out."

Rossi smiled. "He's a coony old bastard, isn't he? I was watching him in the square this morning. You'd think he was running for alderman; smooth as syrup with the other gooks. I wonder where he got that damned hat? It makes him look like one of the Seven Dwarfs."

"I wouldn't trust him farther than I can throw him, but he seems to get things done."

"I've already told you that as far as the gooks go you can run things any way you like," Rossi said, "but if the old gook or anyone else gets out of line, it's going to be your ass, Charley. Get me the water, will you — it's on the fire in front of the house."

Swenson swung his legs inside the window and came back in a moment with an old teakettle. Rossi wrapped the towel around his waist and began to spread shaving cream over his beard. He picked up his razor but before he applied it to his face he turned around and asked Swenson, "Where you getting your liquor, Charley?"

Swenson was almost caught off base, but he recovered quickly. "Just a few bottles we took away from the gooks. I've been rationing it out to the men. It's pretty foul stuff and I figured you wouldn't want any."

"I don't," Rossi said. "I just wanted to know."

The doctor came around the corner of the hut, carrying his toilet utensils in his upturned helmet.

"You're through early," Rossi said.

The doctor grimaced. "Most of my patients are either getting better or they've died. Matter of fact, I've spent most of the afternoon pulling teeth. Lord, it's incredible what a mess some of their mouths are in." He lined up his soap, razor and shaving cream on top of the cistern and began to strip. Rossi went on shaving.

"I'm going to shove off," Swenson said, sliding off the window sill. "I'll let you know how this gook Kaneshiro works out." Rossi nodded and Swenson left him alone with the doctor.

The doctor doused himself cautiously from the water bucket, flinching at the impact of the cool water. He ruefully patted his paunch, which was white and creased between rolls of fat. "Lord, I'm beginning to put it back on. For a while I thought I was going to go back home looking like one of you young fellows. Lots of exercise, fresh air, the outdoor life. Hell, I guess I'm just getting old and fat."

"You're the worst chowhound in the outfit," Rossi said. "It's a wonder the rest of us aren't starving, the way you go after it."

The doctor stopped anointing his body with soap and looked concerned. "I thought there was plenty of food. I didn't mean to do anyone out of his share."

"I guess we'll make out," Rossi said. "We'll just tell them to send down an extra truckload next time."

64

The doctor looked at Rossi dubiously for a moment and then laughed and went back to his bathing. Rossi finished shaving and sat on the edge of the cistern, facing into the sun.

"What's your man Swenson been up to?" the doctor asked casually. "I've been hearing some funny stories about him."

"What do you mean, funny stories?"

"Liquor," the doctor said, "and maybe women."

"Is that all you've heard?"

"I thought you might like to know that we've got practically a whole Japanese cathouse in the stockade."

"I was going to ask you about that. Are they clapped up?"

"Some of them are, but at least a couple of them are clean as a whistle."

"You seem to know a lot about them."

"It's my business to know things like that."

"Does Swenson know which ones are clean?"

"Yes."

"How come you told him?"

"I'm a doctor, not a chaplain. If your men are going to get mixed up with these women it's my business to see that they don't get sick. That doesn't mean I approve of it. I don't."

"I don't either," Rossi said. "I don't give a damn if the men get a piece of tail or not, but I don't like their getting mixed up with the gooks. If this thing gets out of hand, I'm going to wake up some morning and find that the whole platoon is shot to hell. On the other hand, the way the men are feeling now, it'd probably make things worse if I tried to stop them."

"I don't see that. Why don't you just call Swenson in and give him the word?"

"Because, if I did, he'd go ahead anyway, and then he'd know he was putting something over on me. Officially, he already has the word. Unofficially, he knows I know he's been cooking up something. It makes him nervous and he's going to be damn careful he doesn't get too far out of line."

"What *are* you going to do about it?"

"Not a damn thing, not yet at any rate."

"How far are you going to let it go?"

"I'll know when to lower the boom," Rossi said. "You can tell when something like this is beginning to get dangerous. It's not anything anyone says. You smell it. The time to nail it is when you get that first whiff, not after it really begins to stink."

"That may be so but I still don't like it," the doctor said.

"Aren't you taking this pretty hard? The platoon's my business; as far as the gook women go, this isn't a Sunday school."

The doctor took up his towel and dried his head and face. He patted the back of his neck gently; the sunburn was still painful.

"You know," he said, "when I was younger, I taught a Sunday school class. I've changed some of my ideas since then, but it seems to me that you can't ignore the moral aspects of the situation. Those girls won't be sleeping with your men because they like it. They're doing it because they can get something for it: cigarettes, a bar of soap, maybe some extra chow."

"Isn't that the way whores usually operate?" Rossi asked. "Besides, how do you know they don't like it?"

The doctor shrugged. "We're not communicating very well."

"I guess we aren't," Rossi said. "The trouble with you, Doc, is, you're still a civilian."

"Well, if I am, I'm proud of it," the doctor said. "Maybe I'm just being stupid again, but I thought the Marine Corps had

66

regulations to cover this sort of thing. I thought you were supposed to keep discipline in your platoon."

Rossi had gotten to his feet and was taking a pair of clean skivvies from the branch of a tree where they had been drying. He pulled the green T shirt over his head and tucked the tail inside the green shorts before he answered.

"I do keep discipline, but it's not the kind of discipline you read about in books. If I tried to run my platoon according to the book, my men couldn't wait for a chance to do me in. Oh, they'd toe the line all right for a while, but the first time I made a mistake, the platoon would blow up like a firecracker. As I see it, the trick is to let them dope off a bit when they get a chance, but let them know all the time that they're doping off with my permission. The trouble begins if they find out they can get away with something I don't know about."

The doctor lathered his cheeks, using the remainder of the water from the teakettle, now lukewarm. "What about the stockade? How are you planning to keep the prisoners in line? My God, Rossi, sometimes I wake up in a sweat thinking what those gooks could do if they got organized."

"I wouldn't worry about it. What would you do if you had a cage full of five thousand wild animals? You can't talk to them and they don't think the same way you do. So you build a cage that's strong enough to keep them from getting out and you feed them just enough to keep them alive but not enough to let them get too strong for you. And when you go into the cage, you don't turn your back when you're in reach of their claws."

The doctor hacked away doggedly at the stubble on his cheeks. He drew blood once and dabbed at it with the edge of his towel. "How does this work out in practice?"

"It works out," Rossi said, "because we all carry whips. You can't see them but they're there just the same. You even carry one to use on Loomis, but you don't use it often enough. I only need a small one for Swenson; he's a well-trained animal and I just have to flick him with the end of it to make him jump. Swenson has a couple of whips of his own — one for the marines and one for the gooks. But even the one for the gooks doesn't have to be very big. He's already handed out whips to some of the gooks — Kaneshiro and those characters he calls his headmen. Now see what happens: Let's say a stupid little gook way over in the northwest corner of the stockade tries to get away with somebody else's rice ration. Let's say I find out about it. I crack my whip on Swenson, but lightly; Swenson uses his whip on Kaneshiro; Kaneshiro whips one of the headmen; the headman whips somebody below him. It goes on down the line until somebody whales the be-jesus out of the gook who stole the rice."

"Passing the buck," the doctor suggested.

"No," Rossi said, "it's not the same thing at all. Passing the buck keeps things from getting done. This way you get things done, and get them done in a hurry."

A file of Okinawans from one of the working parties straggled down the road and looked curiously through the bushes at the two men at the cistern. One of the Okinawans grinned and bowed jerkily toward the doctor, who lifted his free hand in salute.

"Friend of yours?"

"That man had a nasty infection in his thigh. It cleared up like that," he snapped his fingers, "with sulfa powder." He watched the Okinawans until they were out of sight. "I get a kick out of things like that. Guess that's why I'm a doctor." He splashed water on his face and wiped away the excess shaving cream.

68

"Tell me something. What would happen if Swenson used his whip without your knowing? Suppose he made a mistake and used it on someone who didn't deserve it. What would you do if you found out about it?"

"Not a damn thing. That would wreck the system."

"Lucky Swenson," the doctor said. "He can't do any wrong."

Rossi laughed. "He can do a lot of wrong, and he does, but the only time I'd really lower the boom on him would be if he'd done something that ruined the whole setup. That would be the end of Swenson. I'd have to get a new sergeant and start from scratch."

"Did you figure this out for yourself?"

"Well, it seems to me to be the way things work out. Any officer who's worth a damn operates the same way. The only difference is that if you smile when you crack the whip, you're a good joe; if you look solemn, you're a chickenshit son of a bitch."

The doctor wrapped his towel around his middle, threw his soap and razor into his helmet, and went around the corner of the house. He appeared a moment later in the window, buttoning on a clean but wrinkled shirt. Rossi was sitting in the sun again, smoking a cigarette.

"What happens," the doctor asked, "if you whip a man to the point where he'd rather fight back than get beaten any more?"

"In that case," Rossi said, "somebody's made a mistake."

Seven

THE party was getting under way much too slowly for Swenson. He sat cross-legged on a thin straw mat that had been rolled over the floor boards of the Madame's hut. Beside him Mike conversed discreetly with the Madame, who sat opposite the two men, presiding over a kettle that was simmering on a small charcoal burner. She had changed her daytime outfit of blue for a sober gray kimono and her hair had been heavily pomaded and coiled into a massive coiffure. A coating of thick white powder masked the usually amiable expression of her face.

The kettle began to boil vigorously and the Madame took it from the fire and filled a china pot. She set three cups on the heavy tray by her side and filled them with a thin green tea, drawing the voluminous sleeve of her kimono out of the way as she poured. Swenson accepted a cup and promptly burned his tongue with the scalding liquid. He put his teacup on the floor and stretched his legs, which were beginning to go numb.

The Madame noticed his discomfort and inquired solicitously as to what was troubling him. Mike explained and she brought a thin cushion from a closet and offered it to Swenson.

"Thank you," he said grudgingly.

"*Arigato*," the Madame said.

"You're suppose to say *arigato*," Mike prompted Swenson.

"*Arigato*," said Swenson.

The Madame laughed graciously and settled down again to her conversation with Mike. Swenson sipped his tea miserably.

"She wants to know how Lieutenant Rossi is," Mike said.

"Rossi's all right," Swenson answered. "What does she care how Rossi is?"

The Madame smiled archly. "She says, why don't you bring Rossi with you next time? She thinks he works too hard and a little bit of relaxation wouldn't do him any harm."

"Now look: I've told her before to lay off Rossi. What's she trying to do, give me a bad time?"

"Take it easy, she's just making conversation. Don't you know enough to be polite?"

"Polite?" Swenson groaned. "This is the goddamndest whorehouse I've ever been in. Where the hell are the girls?"

"They'll come. Keep your pants on."

"Why doesn't she just bring them in? I didn't know this was going to be a tea party."

"This is a respectable place," Mike said, grinning. "It isn't one of the two-bit houses you're used to."

"Blow it out the other end," Swenson growled. "You two may be having a high old time banging ears but my ass is about broken from these floor boards." He shifted his position again, juggling the hot teacup from one hand to the other. "What about the liquor?"

"I guess Kaneshiro didn't show," Mike said.

"Oh, God!" Swenson said grimly. "When I catch that bastard Kaneshiro I'm going to break his goddamn neck for him."

He again found himself out of the conversation. Eventually he was forced to accept another cup of tea, which he nursed in gloomy silence. He had smoked three cigarettes and had almost finished the tea when there was a clattering outside the house. Swenson turned expectantly and saw Kaneshiro, full of apologies, bowing and scraping at the door. In his hand was a jug of liquor.

The Madame went to the door, her hand outstretched, but Kaneshiro retained his hold on the earthenware jug and broke into a flood of Japanese, his gruff old voice rising into a whining complaint. The Madame attempted to placate him but he cut her off and his bitter tirade went on. Mike joined in the conversation, sweeping a hand around the room as if to show that this was all there was: Swenson, the Madame, and himself; a charcoal burner and a pot of tea; a tray and three teacups and a guttering candle in a saucer. The old man looked where Mike pointed, peering into the room where the light flickered on the bare boards of the walls.

He was still not satisfied and came into the room. His shadow danced across the ceiling as he shuffled about the room in his bare feet, the jug still in his hand. He examined each dark corner carefully, sniffing like a restless dog. He opened the sliding door of the closet and poked inside but found only a heap of quilts.

"Sit down and have a drink," Swenson said.

"Okay." Kaneshiro relinquished his hold on the jug and knelt on the floor beside Swenson. The Madame rinsed out the teacups with boiling water from the kettle and filled them with the yellowish liquor.

"Bottoms up," Kaneshiro said.

"Bottoms up," Swenson answered.

The Madame refilled their cups.

"What are you looking for?"

"The girl, my niece," Kaneshiro said in English but he was looking at the Madame. She returned his gaze calmly.

72

"She isn't here," Swenson said. "You've looked around; there's just Mike and me and the Madame. What makes you think your niece is here? I haven't even seen the girl for a couple of days."

"Okay," Kaneshiro said, "okay." He tossed off his drink and got to his feet and left without another word. Nobody spoke until the sound of his footsteps had died away.

"Well," Swenson said. "Where *is* his niece?"

His question went unanswered. The Madame laughed and made a spitting sound.

"She says he's a stupid old man."

The Madame took up the jug and filled the men's cups. She rinsed out Kaneshiro's cup and left it empty. Mike took the jug from her and filled the empty cup also. The atmosphere became more genial and the Madame accepted a cigarette, which she smoked fastidiously, holding it between her thumb and forefinger and blowing the smoke out through delicately pursed lips. She filled the men's cups when they were empty and Mike attended to hers, and then the ritual was repeated. The color rose to the Madame's face under the starchy rice powder.

She arose and beckoned to Swenson.

"What's up?" Swenson demanded. "Where's she going to go?"

"Go on. She wants to play a game."

Swenson joined the Madame in the center of the floor. Facing him, the Madame placed her hands on his waist and swung him around, indicating that he was to remain in that position. Then she turned around herself and stood so that they were back-to-back, with about a foot between them.

"What happens now?"

"You'll see," Mike promised.

The Madame suddenly doubled up like a jackknife, thrusting

73

her posterior at Swenson's rear. She caught him across the lower thighs. Swenson's knees buckled and he lost his balance and fell

"Hey, what's the big idea?" he protested.

Giggling, the Madame helped him to his feet.

"You're supposed to throw her before she throws you," Mike explained.

Swenson and the Madame took up their positions again. Swenson took the initiative but the Madame agilely eluded his thrusts. When the force of his attack was spent, she struck again, expertly. Swenson rocked on his toes for a moment before a second blow sent him to the floor. When Swenson had been thrown for the third time the Madame took pity on him and allowed him to rest.

"That's a hell of a game," Swenson said. "How'm I supposed to tell when she's going to hit me?"

"You tried too hard. She just waited till you got yourself off balance and then it didn't take much to knock you down."

The Madame pressed a full cup of liquor on Swenson, who accepted it gratefully. "I'll tell you this, lady, you sure beat the be-jesus out of me." The Madame smiled as if she understood. "But, look, I didn't come here to play that sort of game. How about the girls?"

The Madame raised her eyebrows inquiringly and Mike interpreted.

"Ah," the Madame said, "*pom-pom?*"

"That's the idea. *Pom-pom.*"

The Madame excused herself and left the house, slipping away silently on straw sandals.

Swenson peered into the liquor jug. "This party can't last much longer; we're getting low on liquor. You don't figure she's run out on us, do you?"

"She'll be back," Mike said. He leaned back against the wall and stretched out his legs. He unbuttoned his fatigue jacket and flapped the sides back and forth to make a breeze across his chest. There were flushed patches on the skin of his face, around his eyes and on each cheek.

"That stuff makes me hot," he said crossly.

"You haven't had enough to make a twelve-year-old kid drunk. I guess old Gunny Cook was right. Gunny claimed he hadn't met a gook yet that wasn't a thimble-belly."

"Who's a gook?"

"You're a gook."

"Who says I'm a gook?"

"I say you're a gook and a thimble-belly."

"Goddammit," Mike said, "I've told you once I don't have to take any crap from you." He started to get to his feet but thought better of it and fell back again against the wall. "You stupid Swede, Charley, you don't know sugar from Shinola."

"Ah, screw you," Swenson said.

"Screw you too," Mike answered. He began to laugh and Swenson laughed with him.

The Madame returned as quietly as she had left. With her were two girls. They knelt at the doorway and bowed before entering the room. The Madame resumed her former seat, the girls flanking her.

The girl on the Madame's left was a bold wench with a hard, knowing face. She was as thin as an alley cat and her shoulder bones showed through the thin cloth of her faded kimono. Her hair had been clipped in a short bob, which she shook wantonly at Swenson's frank appraisal of her.

The other girl was Kaneshiro's niece. She sat demurely by the Madame, her eyes cast down on the floor. Belying her bashful manner, her round face was flushed with excitement. She glanced quickly at Swenson and turned her face away and giggled into the sleeve of her kimono. She was young and plump and pretty and Swenson knew that he wanted her.

"Come here, Peggy," he said.

The girl slid across the floor to his side. Mike leered drunkenly at the other girl. "I guess you're mine, Judy, you old bitch," he said in English and then went into Japanese.

Each time Swenson emptied his teacup, Peggy refilled it from the liquor jug. Except for Swenson's "*Arigato*" they were, of necessity, silent. Swenson put his arm around the girl's waist and she permitted it to remain there. He toyed with the *obi* that held her kimono together but she restrained him from exploring deeper than the first layer of cloth. The Madame smiled, tolerant of the girl's modesty, and loosened her own kimono so that the air could penetrate to her body. Her coiffure was askew and the heavy makeup on her face was streaked with sweat. She closed her eyes and lifted her voice in song, a melancholy air with a monotonous refrain in which the girls joined, clapping their hands in time to the rhythm. Mike added his voice to the last chorus.

"Very nice," Swenson said, "very nice. Now I'll sing one." He took a swig of whisky and began to sing in a mincing cockney accent.

> *Oh, I don't want to be a soldier,*
> *I don't want to go to war.*
> *I just want to hang around*
> *Piccadilly Underground,*
> *Living off the earnings of an 'igh-born lydie.*

His voice was hoarse and dry and he was moved to refresh himself with a full cup of whisky. Peggy and Judy clapped their hands politely. Swenson protested indignantly that he wasn't through yet.

> *I don't want a bay'net up me arse-'ole;*
> *I don't want me buttocks shot aw'y.*
> *I want to st'y in England,*
> *In merry, merry England,*
> *And roger all my friggin' life aw'y,*
> *Gorrr-blimey!*

A rock crashed against the wall. Swenson clambered to his feet and went to the window.

"Who the hell's making that racket?" he roared.

Fischer's voice came through the trees. "For Christ's sake, Charley, knock it off. You'll have the lieutenant up here with your damned howling."

"Get back to your post! If I catch you goofing off again, I'm going to — "

"I'm at my post. If you want to make something of it, I'll turn you in right now."

Swenson thought for a while. "Ah, relax, meathead. I'm coming out."

He crashed through the trees toward the place where Fischer stood guard outside the fence. Fischer's post looked down on the stockade from the rear. It was far from the main gate and isolated; a nervous man could hear enemy infiltrators crawling about all night long.

"You sure got a load on. You came through those trees like a herd of elephants," Fischer observed.

77

"I'm all right," Swenson said. "What's eating you?"

"It's that goddamn singing, Charley. I can't pretend I don't hear it and it sure don't sound like any gook singing. What happens if the lieutenant hears you?"

"You're right. I wouldn't want to get you in trouble," Swenson said with an air of benevolence.

"Me in trouble! Hell!"

There was a pause.

"You know, meathead, I've got a girl all picked out for you. Looks like Hedy Lamarr."

"Stop snowing me," Fischer protested. "I ain't seen no Hedy Lamarr in this stockade. All I want is a little gook girl. How do I know you're not going to hold out on me?"

"I'm looking out for you. I've never crossed you up yet, have I?"

"I don't know," Fischer said, "you've pulled some funny deals. You've been putting me off for damn near a week now."

"I'm looking out for you," Swenson repeated. "You just take it easy and you'll get yours."

Fischer lifted his rifle and fingered the operating handle. "You know, Charley, if I was to follow my orders I could plug you right now and nobody would do a thing to me. For all I can tell in the dark you might be a gook trying to sneak through the wire."

"Put that goddamn rifle down," Swenson ordered. "You pull anything like that again and I'll fix it so you won't be interested in seeing any women here or anywhere else."

Fischer laughed uncertainly and put down his rifle.

"You're the most trigger-happy bastard I've ever seen," Swenson said. "I'm getting out of here before you blow both our heads off."

78

Swenson returned to the house and the girls and the liquor. "Fischer's getting nervous," he told Mike. "We got to quit making so goddamn much noise." He took up his song where it had been interrupted, croaking in a hoarse whisper.

> *Call out the Army and the Ny-vee,*
> *Call out the rank and the file,*
> *Call out the loyal Terri-torials,*
> *They'll fyce dynger with a smile,*
> *Gorrr-blimey!*
> *Call out the members of the old brigyde,*
> *They'll keep England free.*
> *Call out me brother,*
> *Me sister and me mother,*
> *But for God's sake, don't call me!*

The end of the song was greeted with applause. "I learned that bloody song," Swenson announced, "from the bloody Austrylians, who don't have no bloody use for the bloody English. Oh, bloody, bloody, bloody!"

He mopped his fiery face with the sleeve of his jacket while Peggy filled his cup. He was draining the last of the liquor when another song came from farther up the hill. It was a plaintive song without a melody one could follow, and while it lasted there was silence in the room. The Madame and the girls listened with fixed smiles until it died away.

"The crazy bloody gee-sha," Swenson said. He laughed but none of the others joined him. The Madame was toying with an errant lock of hair, attempting to re-form it into a neat coil, while the girls fidgeted uneasily. Mike lolled against the wall, staring at the ceiling with glassy eyes.

Swenson shook Mike. "Come out of it, Junior, you look like

you're about to pass out." Mike blinked and smiled slowly. "That's better. Ask the Madame what's the poop on that crazy gee-sha."

Mike frowned with the effort of concentrating on phrasing the question. The Madame continued to adjust her coiffure while she answered. "She says the gee-sha was the general's mistress. He brought her all the way from Tokyo with him. She went along with him on the retreat down south. The last time the Madame saw her she was living with the general in the headquarters cave. She was all right then; she must have cracked up some time after that." The strain of conducting a conversation was too much for Mike. He collapsed slowly onto the floor, where he lay in peace, breathing heavily. His girl, Judy, took alarm and attempted to revive him. She took his head in her lap and stroked his forehead, but he only groaned and buried his head deeper in the skirt of her kimono.

"That's all for him tonight, girlie," Swenson said. "One down, four to go. Come on, what's the matter with you all?" He squinted into the jug. "Just enough for one more round."

He pressed a cup on Peggy, who drank it in little, birdlike sips, giggling in spite of her grimaces of distaste. The Madame tossed off a full cup and her spirits seemed to revive immediately. Only Judy refused to respond to Swenson's efforts and continued to gaze forlornly at Mike's prostrate body. Swenson turned the jug upside down. A single drop of liquor fell from its lip.

"That's all there is, there ain't no more," Swenson chanted.

The Madame nodded and went to the closet. She pulled out a mound of cotton quilts and with the girls' help began to lay them out on the floor. They made two neat pallets, one against each wall.

Swenson dragged Mike across the floor and stretched him

out on one of the pallets. The Madame took off Mike's jacket while Swenson tugged at his pants. At last Mike lay naked except for his undershorts, his thin, brown body curled up like a child's in a deep sleep. The Madame leered at Swenson, took up her candle, and went to the door. Judy, after a last look at Mike, reluctantly followed her.

Swenson reached out an arm toward Peggy but she pulled away from him with a giggle. He waited and in the darkness he could hear the rustling sound of her kimono's being undone. He started to grope his way across the floor toward the sound but thought better of it and changed his course for the window.

He searched the darkness outside for a moment, straining for a clue as to where Fischer was keeping guard. There were only the dim outlines of the treetops against the starlit sky. He gave up the attempt to fix Fischer's position precisely and cupped his hands around his mouth.

"Pull up the ladder, mate!" he sang out. "Swenson's aboard!"

Eight

"ARE you sure you know where you're going, Corcoran?" Tom Witherspoon asked, a bit querulously. He grabbed for the handle on the side of the jeep as Corcoran bounced them over a hummock on the rutted road.

"Don't get your ass in an uproar, Lieutenant," Corcoran said calmly and settled down to a steady twenty-five miles an hour. Witherspoon released the handle and felt under the seat for his dictionaries. The bulky Japanese-English dictionary had been thrown to the rear of the jeep where it lay with a smear of mud across its open pages. Witherspoon retrieved it and held it in his lap while he continued his search until he had found a smaller book that was wedged between his seat and the side of the jeep.

Corcoran swung the jeep over the ruts onto a side road that pointed toward the mountain. Witherspoon hung on with one hand and grasped his dictionaries firmly with the other. They roared along a straightaway until Corcoran tramped on the brake pedal and pulled up by a six-by-six that was parked by the side of the road. He hailed a stunted black marine who was sitting on the running board of the truck, drinking from a canteen.

"Say, Mac, is there a stockade full of gooks down this road?" The Negro put away the canteen and came over to the jeep.

"You should have turned off back at the last road. You go about two miles along that road and you'll see it off to your right along the side of the mountain. You can't miss it."

Corcoran drew ahead of the truck and turned the jeep around. When they drove back the Negro was waiting for them.

"If you think you're going to get yourselves a piece of tail," he called, "you'd better turn around real quick. That lieutenant up there is sort of chickenshit, at least that's what they tell me."

After they had passed the truck Corcoran grinned at Witherspoon. "That poor jigaboo probably thought you were a pfc, Lieutenant. You should have chewed his ass out."

Witherspoon felt absently at the collar of his dungaree jacket. He was used to having his status misinterpreted when he wasn't wearing insignia. "That's all right," he said. "I don't give a damn."

They found the stockade by following the Negro marine's directions. On the left side of the road, opposite the stockade, were several huts surrounding a clearing with shade trees. In front of one of the huts a tall, dark-haired marine was sitting on an empty box, eating square crackers spread thickly with raspberry jam.

Witherspoon got out of the jeep. "I'm looking for Lieutenant Rossi."

"I'm Rossi. What are you after?"

"My name's Witherspoon. I'm a language officer from Division."

Rossi motioned him to sit on another box. "Have some breakfast? One of my men scrounged me some ten-in-ones last night."

Witherspoon took a cracker and bit into the sweet, sticky raspberry pulp.

"Coffee?" Rossi handed him a steaming canteen cup.

"You're pretty well set up here," Witherspoon said.

"We make out."

Corcoran wandered over to the main gate and peered between the wire at the women washing clothes inside. A file of Okinawans came up the road, bent under loads of corrugated iron and scrap lumber. They turned into the stockade and Corcoran followed them through the gate.

"Did you come down to talk to the gooks?"

"In a way," Witherspoon admitted. "The colonel wants me to track down the last Japanese C.P."

"What in hell does he want to do that for?"

"The colonel has a theory that the Japanese commander got off by submarine. The navy reported some lights flashing off the southern coast last week, but by the time a picket boat got down there whatever it was had taken off. The colonel's upset about it and he's ready to raise hell if the navy let General Matsui get away by submarine."

"If the poor bastard got out alive, he probably had to commit Harry Cary anyway."

"Hara-kiri," Witherspoon said. "You're probably right but the colonel wants to make sure. He'd like some proof that Matsui didn't get away. If we could find his body, for instance."

"Who the hell's this colonel?"

"Colonel Smith, D-2."

"*That* son of a bitch. What does he want, souvenirs? Every time anybody comes down from Division they hang around until somebody gives them a sword or a pistol for some goddamn colonel. It wouldn't be so bad if they were the only ones. I damn near got my tail shot off crawling around a cave with a chaplain. He claimed he'd played tackle for Notre Dame and wanted something to send back to Father Somebody-or-other."

84

"As a matter of fact, I understand that General Marsh would like to get hold of Matsui's sword."

"Well, what do you want me to do for you?"

"I want a guide to take me down south. The Japanese built their C.P.'s underground with civilian labor gangs. I think there's probably somebody here who helped dig the caves."

"You figuring on going alone? You and your driver?"

"Colonel Smith told me I could pick up some men from you."

"What does this colonel think I'm running? My men have better things to do than chase around after dead Japs."

"I guess Corcoran and I'll go down alone."

Rossi laughed. "What would you do if you ran into a Jap? Beat him to death with your dictionary?"

Witherspoon flushed and tightened his grip on his books.

"I'd just as soon get out of here myself for a while," Rossi said equably. He called to the guard at the gate. "Pass the word to Mike to drag his ass down here on the double."

The cry was taken up inside the stockade. In a few minutes Mike came through the gate.

"This officer has a job for you," Rossi said. "You do what he tells you."

Witherspoon explained what he was after. Mike nodded. He lingered for a moment, his eyes on the dictionary Witherspoon was still holding.

"You speak Japanese, sir?"

"Yes," Witherspoon said. "Yes, I speak Japanese."

"You use that dictionary when you speak Japanese, sir?"

"No."

"You just carry it around because you like it, sir?"

"Get the hell out of here, Mike," Rossi ordered. "The lieutenant didn't come here to argue with you. Pick up Davis and

Taliaferro when you come back. You can tell Swenson that I'm going to need them for a couple of hours."

Mike came back with a young, surly-faced prisoner. They were followed by Davis and Taliaferro. Corcoran strolled over from the gate.

"His name's Harada," Mike said. "He says he's an Okinawan but I think he's a Jap deserter myself. Look at him, he's no Okinawan. He's a goddamn Jap but he won't admit it."

Witherspoon spoke to Harada in halting Japanese. Harada did not understand him. He shook his head, looked at Mike, and shrugged.

"What's the matter?" Rossi asked. "Does he talk a different dialect or something?"

Witherspoon began again. Harada stared blankly toward the top of the mountain. Mike clouted him lightly on the shoulder. "*Nihongo da zo, bakayaro!*"

Harada's face showed amazement and then sudden comprehension.

"*Ah, Nihongo,*" he said, smiling broadly. He listened to Witherspoon with exaggerated attention and answered slowly and distinctly, forming his words as if he were talking to a backward child or a lip reader. When he was through, he made a digging motion and rubbed the small of his back, meanwhile groaning excruciatingly.

"What does he say?" Rossi asked.

"I think he may be our man," Witherspoon said. "He worked in a cave for the Japs."

"I could have told you that and I don't need a dictionary to understand him. You come along, Mike, Lieutenant Witherspoon may need your help." Rossi pushed Harada toward the jeep. "Come on, Tojo. Let's get this show on the road."

86

They drove south, skirting the mountain, past a Seabee camp and three crumpled radio masts. Witherspoon and Corcoran rode ahead, with the prisoner and Davis in the back seat. Rossi, Mike, and Taliaferro followed them in a second jeep. Witherspoon's jeep kicked up such a cloud of yellow dust that Mike, who was driving the second jeep, kept a hundred yards behind, where the atmosphere was still thick but not intolerable.

Davis pulled out a pack of cigarettes and lighted one, bending toward the floor of the jeep and catching the first flare of the match. When his cigarette was going, he offered the pack to Harada.

"You want a smoke, Tojo?"

Harada took the cigarette and rolled it tenderly between his fingers before he lighted it.

"You give the gook a cigarette?" Corcoran asked.

"Sure," Davis said. "Why not?"

"I'd be damned if I'd give a gook a cigarette."

"It's my cigarette."

"Okay, okay, don't get your ass in an uproar."

"Shut up," Witherspoon said mildly.

"I didn't say anything, Lieutenant."

"All right. Just keep your eyes on the road."

"I'm watching the road, Lieutenant. Don't get your ass in an uproar."

"Oh, shut up," Witherspoon said.

Harada sat quietly in the back seat, smoking greedily and watching the road closely. On one side was a jungle of trees and brush, and on the other the mountain sloped off sharply to the sea. In front of them the road descended onto the long, flat expanse of cane fields, which were slashed diagonally across by the raw earth of the new airstrip. Beyond the airstrip were more cane fields and then the escarpment. The escarpment cut across the island from east to west, lifting the southern third of the island onto a plateau. The plateau was bounded by cliffs that dropped fifty feet to the rocks where the green tide boiled in and rose in angry shafts of spray.

There were other vehicles on the road now — jeeps, weapons carriers, six-by-sixes, and a single duck — each one spewing up a great yellow cloud that drifted slowly inland on the sea breeze. The dust clung to Witherspoon's face like a mask, working under his eyelids and caking on his lips.

They stopped once to let Harada relieve himself and then they kept going toward the escarpment until they were in a wilder, less traveled part of the island, where the road was sometimes constricted by the wreck of a burned-out tank and where the occasional Japanese corpses along the way were relatively fresh and even recognizably human. When they were almost within the shadow of the escarpment they were hailed by a marine who was cleaning a machine gun mounted inside a circle of sandbags. The machine gunner came out from behind the sandbags and approached Witherspoon's jeep.

"Where the hell do you think you're going with that gook?"

"We're from D-2," Witherspoon said.

"That gook from Division, too?"

"Well, not exactly."

"What's the trouble?" Rossi demanded from the rear jeep. "What the hell's holding you up?"

The machine gunner glanced at Rossi and then goggled at Mike. "My God, another gook! What's going on at Division, anyway?"

"Take it easy," Rossi said. "He's a dogface."

88

"A doggie," the machine gunner said, with evident disappointment. "What's a gook doing in the army?"

"The army's full of gooks," Rossi told him soberly. "They got a million of them. A whole goddamn Jap corps surrendered on New Guinea so they put them all in the army. Is there an officer around here?"

The machine gunner pointed to a clump of trees off the road. "The captain's crapped out in there. He's not going to like it if you wake him up."

"I'll take a chance on that."

The machine gunner stared at Mike for a while. Finally he turned to Taliaferro. "This gook speak American?"

"Why don't you ask him?"

"You speak American?"

Mike stared back inscrutably.

"What's the scoop?" the machine gunner demanded. "What's his gook doing in a doggie uniform? How's he get along if he don't speak American?"

"Why don't you ask him?"

"Ah, wise guy." He turned back to Mike. "Tojo. Hirohito. *Banzai*. Harry Cary. You understand that?"

Mike flicked his cigarette butt neatly at the machine gunner's feet. "Go blow it out your ass," he recommended.

Fortunately, Rossi returned at this moment. The machine gunner backed away, muttering dark threats. Rossi stopped at Witherspoon's jeep.

"This captain claims there are half a dozen big caves along the west coast. What does Tojo know about them?"

Witherspoon consulted with Harada. "He seems to be confused. I think that what he's trying to say is that he'd know the cave if he saw it, but he's not sure how to get there."

89

"Jesus Christ!" Rossi said. "Jesus H. Christ! We could have left the bastard at home."

Rossi got into his jeep and pulled ahead of Witherspoon. He led them up the steep trail which had been bulldozed through a break in the sheer wall of the escarpment and which continued through the jungle on the western edge of the plateau. After they had gone the better part of a mile Harada insisted on stopping.

"He says he'd rather go on foot," Witherspoon told Rossi. "The country's beginning to look familiar to him and he's afraid we might run past the cave in the jeep."

"All right, you stick with Tojo, Davis. If there's any monkey business, shoot him and we'll all get the hell out of here."

Harada and Davis went ahead on foot, with the jeeps crawling behind. At one point, Harada stooped down and picked up an object from the side of the road. He showed Davis a Japanese grenade, a small, black, cast-iron cylinder, surmounted by a smaller brass cap pierced by a pin. Davis snatched it from him and heaved it off into the jungle. Then he marched Harada back to the jeeps, prodding him on with the muzzle of his rifle.

"I would have let him have it if he'd looked like he was going to pull the pin."

"Ask him what the hell he thought he was doing."

Witherspoon conferred with Harada. "He thought Davis might want it for a souvenir."

"Tell him we'll get our own souvenirs. You might let him know that Davis has orders to shoot him if he gets any more ideas like that."

Witherspoon translated this speech in a mild, half-apologetic tone, and Harada, looking sullen, marched off again with Davis.

After another quarter of a mile, Harada led Davis off the

oad onto a trail through the scrub. Davis stopped him and
waited until the others had caught up. The trail ended suddenly
in a heap of red dirt that was piled against a depression in the
side of a low hill. Harada chattered rapidly to Witherspoon.

"What does the gook say?" Rossi asked.

"I don't quite get it." Witherspoon began talking with Harada
again but Mike broke in.

"He says this is it. One of the entrances is under that pile of
dirt. The cave goes back into the hill for about two hundred
yards."

Rossi sent Taliaferro to the top of the hill, where he squatted
with his BAR. Corcoran remained with the jeeps. Mike scrambled to the top of the mound of loose dirt and began to dig it
away with an entrenching tool. The dirt was fresh and still damp
from the early morning rain.

"They did a good job," Mike reported. "Looks like somebody
brought down the whole front of the cave with a satchel charge.
They weren't taking any chances on the Japs getting out."

"Give your shovel to Tojo. We might as well get some work
out of him."

Harada worked steadily and he had soon made visible progress. He stopped once and accepted a cigarette from Witherspoon. After five or six puffs he stubbed it out and put the butt
behind his ear. Finally the blade of the shovel found the roof of
the entrance to the cave. Harada scooped up two more shovel
loads and there was an opening large enough to put one's head
into. Rossi turned a flashlight into the hole. Nothing happened
and after a short wait he peered inside.

Rossi handed the flashlight to Witherspoon. A cool current
of moist air, tainted with a heavy, putrid odor, blew against
Witherspoon's face. The light showed an incline of the same

91

soft dirt that was on the outside, sloping into a large chamber, the floor of which was well below ground level. The chamber was empty except for two wooden cartons and an empty straw bag lying against one wall. At the end of the chamber there was the entrance to a low corridor.

"At least there's some ventilation," Witherspoon said.

"Must be another entrance. We'll let it air out for a while."

Rossi and Witherspoon sat on the ground at one side while Harada enlarged the hole.

"You're pretty sure this is the right cave?"

"Well, Harada seems to know what he's talking about. We had some reports that the Japanese had set up their headquarters around here somewhere. I don't suppose we'll know for sure until we go in."

"Now, let me get this straight. What are we looking for?"

"First of all, we want to find General Matsui's body. If we don't, we'd like any other evidence that would bear on whether he got away or not. In any case, I want to pick up any documents we run across."

"Documents?"

"Papers. Orders, records, maps — anything of that sort."

"You been in many caves before?"

"This is the first time; as a matter of fact, it's the first time I've gotten away from the C.P."

"Let's see your forty-five."

Witherspoon handed over the pistol. Rossi slipped the magazine out and tested the action. "I'm going to take this," he said, snapping the magazine into place and putting a round into the chamber.

"What about me?"

"We'll take care of you. You can take my carbine if you want but it'll probably only get in your way. Now, when we go in, I'm sending Tojo and Mike first, then me, then you. Davis will bring up the rear. Don't touch anything unless I tell you to. We only brought two flashlights. I'm going to take one and you can have the other."

"All right. The pistol would be just a nuisance anyway. I'll want my hands free if we find anything." As a matter of fact, Witherspoon was vastly relieved that Rossi had disarmed him. Firearms filled him with an uneasiness such as might be experienced by a man who was forced to carry a live rattlesnake in his hip pocket.

Rossi slipped through the hole Harada had made and descended the incline, holding Witherspoon's pistol in his right hand and the flashlight in his left. He stood in the entrance to the corridor that led off the first chamber and directed the beam of the flashlight into its depths.

"Come along," he said finally. "It's going to be sort of messy."

They filed in one by one, with Harada in the lead. Harada balked at the entrance to the corridor and Mike had to urge him on with shoves from his carbine and a stream of vigorous Japanese. Rossi fell in behind Mike and then it was Witherspoon's turn.

Witherspoon saw a wide ledge cut into the side of the corridor. There were bodies on the ledge, lying shoulder to shoulder in a single rank with their heavy boots hanging over the edge. They were dressed in full uniform, including insignia and service ribbons, and their swords leaned against the wall at their heads. Witherspoon let his light linger for a moment on one of the faces. The eye sockets were filled with a mass of putrefaction and the swollen black lips were drawn back over yellow teeth. He lowered the beam of his light onto a belly torn open

93

by a hand grenade, a cavity of white bone and purple meat. Witherspoon quickly swung his light onto the next corpse. This one had disembowelled himself with an angular sword-stroke and had fallen backward still gripping the blade of his long sword. These were the officers; the enlisted men lay, half-submerged in an evil green slime, on the floor of the passageway.

Rossi flashed his light back at Witherspoon. "What's holding you?"

Witherspoon stepped forward gingerly onto the chest of the first body in the passageway. His foot slipped in the slime and he flailed about in a wild panic. When he regained his balance, one of his feet had become wedged between two bodies. He extricated his foot and took another step forward. His nostrils were filled with the stink of corruption, his legs were trembling violently, and his stomach was in outright revolt. He stumbled forward mechanically for half a dozen steps before he began to recover control of himself. After another few steps he found that he could consider dispassionately where to find the firmest foothold.

"You're doing fine, Lieutenant," Davis said. "Think how that gook must feel, stepping on his buddies."

They came out from the corridor into a spacious cavern, covered with a high-domed ceiling of natural rock. Harada, Mike, and Rossi were making their way through a field of leaf-less underground plants. Rossi's flashlight picked out the dead-white, spiky stalks which stood in isolated clumps, as if the farmer who had sowed the crop had dropped his seed carelessly, at random intervals. Witherspoon hurried across a dry stone floor to where Rossi waited. The plants were revealed as a white fungus that grew from the bodies on the floor.

Harada, closely followed by Rossi and Mike, scuttled toward

an entranceway cut through the far wall of the chamber. There had once been a door there, but the wooden beams had rotted and fallen in such a way that there was only enough room for a man to crawl through on his hands and knees.

"Send the gook through first," Rossi said.

Harada and Mike crawled under the obstruction. Rossi passed his flashlight through to them and followed. Witherspoon wriggled through the hole with his flashlight held in front of him. The light struck something solid; when Witherspoon looked up he was staring into a bloated dead face. He lay there for a time with his eyes tightly closed before he deliberately took hold of one of the corpse's arms and dragged himself to a kneeling position.

The small square room in which he found himself had been cut from solid rock. Rossi was crouched on the floor, examining three bodies that were laid out against one wall. Harada and Mike stood in front of an unpainted field desk that faced the entrance. On the desk were four tin cups and an empty bottle of Haig & Haig, arranged on a linen napkin. Beside the bottle was a field telephone. On the wall behind the desk there was a map of the island, printed in pale pastel shades, but with jagged red arrows swooping down from the north and breaching a narrow blue line. In the far corner of the room a number of packing boxes were stacked one on top of the other, reaching nearly to the ceiling. The stream of fresh air that had made the rest of the cave tolerable had not penetrated this far.

Witherspoon joined Rossi in front of the bodies. The first was of a bald man with a thin, severe face. He had committed hara-kiri. He was wearing only a loose white kimono, which had been pulled apart where his belly was slit, but a heavy wool uniform, embellished with red-and-gold collar tabs and three

95

rows of ribbons, hung from a hook driven into the wall behind
him. The second body was that of a young soldier. Whoever
had arranged his body had left in his hand the Luger-type
revolver with which he had put a bullet through his head. Next
to the soldier lay the body of a woman dressed in an old-
fashioned nurse's uniform with a high, stiff collar and long,
flowing skirts. Her throat had been slit from ear to ear.

"Is the old man your general?"

"If that's his uniform, he's a colonel," Witherspoon said.
"The other one's a corporal." He glanced at Harada, who was
standing silently at the colonel's feet.

"Harada!" Witherspoon said sharply. Harada looked up, but
the motion was too stiff, as if he were snapping to attention on
command.

"Watch him, Lieutenant," Mike said. "You'll see he's a Jap
like I told you."

"I'll watch him," Witherspoon said. He looked around the
room with disappointment. "The general must have gotten
away. I suppose this is the remains of his farewell party."

Rossi had crossed the room and was tugging at the boxes that
were piled in the corner. Mike helped him move them aside.
Behind the boxes was a cubicle that was barely wide enough to
contain an iron cot. The body of a portly, gray-haired Japanese,
dressed in a dark-green cotton uniform with gold collar tabs,
lay on the cot. He was at rest; one arm hung easily over the edge
of the cot and touched the naked blade of a long sword that was
lying on the ground. Beside the sword there was a cloth cap
without insignia, a glass vial partly filled with yellow tablets, and
a leather map case stuffed with papers.

"The old bastard took poison," Rossi said. "He didn't have
the guts to kill himself like the rest."

Harada sucked in his breath loudly. He had again stiffened to attention but when Witherspoon spoke to him he didn't respond. The Japanese was crying silently. There were no signs of emotion other than the great tears that were rolling down his face.

"You see, what did I tell you?" Mike said triumphantly. He struck Harada viciously across the face. "*Chikisho!*"

Harada remained at attention but his weeping became audible and convulsive. "Matsui *Chujo!* Matsui *Chujo!*" he sobbed.

"Yes, it's General Matsui all right," Witherspoon said. He knelt on the floor and began to shuffle through the map case while Rossi held a light for him. There was a sharp sound of slapping behind them, followed by a burst of Mike's harsh Japanese.

"Leave him alone," Witherspoon said. "We can't expect him to act as if he enjoyed this."

"Lay off him, Mike," Rossi ordered. "But if the son of a bitch gets an inch out of line, let him have it. Get him away from here. I can't stand his goddamn crying."

Mike took Harada away from the cubicle and turned him over to Davis. "You take him. I'll kill the goddamn Jap if I got to mess around with him."

When Witherspoon was through with the papers he leaned over the body and began to rip the collar tabs from the tunic. "For Colonel Smith," he said. The vile stink of the body hit him full in the face as he bent over to pick at the stitches that held the small gold rectangles to the collar.

Mike sat on the edge of the desk and toyed with the whisky bottle. "Let me take a look around, Lieutenant. Maybe there's some more of this stuff."

97

"Sure," Rossi said. "Sure, go ahead. We might as well have a crack at this souvenir hunting too."

"I don't give a damn. I thought maybe you could use some liquor."

"I said, go ahead. If they're going to send an officer all the way down from Division to pick up souvenirs, we might as well get our licks in too."

"I guess anything I pick up, he'll take back for some colonel at Division."

"You're not just beating your gums."

Witherspoon ignored the conversation. When he was through searching the dead general he picked up the sword and slipped it into its plain black scabbard. "I'm through here," he said. "I've got plenty to show that that's really Matsui." He held up the sword. "This is for General Marsh."

"Aren't you going through these other bodies? You might find something more for Old Brassass if you looked real carefully."

"I think I'd better, if you don't mind. It'll only take a few minutes. I'd like to go through the desk drawers too. Will somebody please take down that map?"

Witherspoon leaned the sword against the desk and began to go through the pockets of the colonel's uniform. They were all empty. He knelt beside the corporal. He was suddenly aware that neither the smell nor the damp feel of the bodies disturbed him any longer. Even Rossi's hostility couldn't shake his mounting self-confidence. He worked rapidly, and as he worked he found that he was noting curious details, such as the heavy Chinese jade ring on the corporal's finger.

It was when he was almost finished with the corporal that he heard a crash of glass and metal on the floor. He swung around and saw Mike on the floor by the desk, pawing for Rossi's flashlight. Something struck him from behind and then there was the jarring report of a forty-five. Witherspoon's light was knocked from his hand and a splinter of rock gashed his cheek.

Witherspoon was never able to reconstruct exactly what happened during the next minute. Afterward, when he attempted to describe what happened to him, he remembered the cold, pulpy flesh of the corpse that guarded the doorway, and a shriek of pain and fear from somebody else in the dark cave where the white fungus grew. Then came a terrified race through the darkness. Sometimes Witherspoon was running blindly, stumbling over the bodies but managing to keep his balance, and at other times he was on his hands and knees, crawling slowly forward through a field of plants that brushed damply against his cheeks and broke off with a brittle snap.

The next thing he remembered clearly was falling into a pool of putrid liquid. He lay there for a moment, feeling the cold liquid seep through his clothes and into his boots. His limbs quivered and a stream of hot urine coursed down the inside of his leg. Through his terror he realized that he had, by blind chance, found the exit to the cave and that he was lying among the corpses in the corridor. Whoever he had followed was splashing through the slime ahead of him. Witherspoon moved forward, lifting himself over a body and falling into the slime and then lifting himself over the next body. The liquid splashed into his nostrils and against his closed eyelids but he moved ahead doggedly, possessed only by the necessity of escaping before his body failed him completely.

His tortuous journey was ended suddenly by a pistol shot from directly in front of him.

"I've got you, you son of a bitch!" a voice cried.

Witherspoon lifted his head and saw a beam of light playing on the floor of the corridor.

"It's me!" he cried. "For Christ's sake!"

The light blinded him.

"My God!" Corcoran's voice said distinctly. "It's the lieutenant."

Corcoran helped Witherspoon through the rest of the passageway, up the incline, and into the sunlight. Witherspoon fell onto the soft ground and retched violently until he lay weak and purged, while Corcoran dabbed at his mouth with a filthy green handkerchief. But the air was cool and clean and the warm sun soothed his twitching muscles. Witherspoon began to take some pleasure in the simple awareness of being alive, and as he revived he realized that he had not been wounded.

"You might have killed me, Corcoran."

"It wasn't you, it was that gook, Tojo. He came charging at me like a bat out of hell. I think I got him in the leg."

Corcoran was festooned with Japanese weapons. Two officer's swords were stuck through his belt, a rifle was slung over his shoulder, and a tremendous pistol was in his pocket. His own pistol was still in his hand. "What happened to the rest?" he asked.

"I don't know," Witherspoon said weakly. "I got separated from them."

Taliaferro's round face appeared over the crest of the hill. "Where the hell's the lieutenant?"

"I don't know," Witherspoon said again.

Taliaferro scrambled down the side of the hill to where Witherspoon lay. "Get rid of that goddamn junk," he ordered Corcoran. "We're going after the lieutenant."

Corcoran threw off the swords and the rifle and pistol; they landed on the ground at Witherspoon's side with a great clatter. Corcoran slid through the hole after Taliaferro and then Witherspoon was alone.

They were gone a long time. Witherspoon fumbled in his pocket for a cigarette, but the pack was damp and the cigarettes disintegrated when he pulled them out. He crawled away from where his vomit was drying on the ground and stretched out again in the sunlight. His nerves had become quieter and he was in a state of not unpleasant weariness. He had done his job, he told himself, he had established that General Matsui had died on the island. There had been no escape to Japan by submarine. Colonel Smith would be pleased. Witherspoon dozed.

He could not have been asleep for more than a few minutes when he awoke painfully. Rossi and the others were still in the cave. The humiliating picture of what had happened was suddenly very clear. Rossi's light had smashed on the floor and in the confusion Harada had broken away. He, Tom Witherspoon, had also fled, following the Japanese and probably preventing Rossi from firing again. He had raised himself to a sitting position and was about to get to his feet before he remembered that Taliaferro and Corcoran had already gone after Rossi.

Witherspoon was assailed by vivid images of what might be going on inside the cave. Even now, Rossi and the others, without his luck, might be stumbling through the darkness toward an underground well or a taut wire rigged to trip off a battery of grenades. The sun had become insufferably hot and Witherspoon's throat was dry and painful. He discovered a bruise on one knee which throbbed cruelly when he touched it. He sat hunched on the ground, his head buried between his knees, and miserably awaited Taliaferro and Corcoran's return.

Rossi was the first to emerge from the cave. He stalked over to Witherspoon and threw the dead general's sword onto the pile of weapons Corcoran had left.

"I brought you your goddamn souvenirs. I see you picked up some more on your way out."

"I'm sorry," Witherspoon said abjectly. He tried to explain that the other weapons were Corcoran's but Rossi didn't hear him. He had turned away and was watching Mike and Davis haul Harada through the entrance to the cave. One leg of Harada's trousers was torn and bloody. They threw him down beside Witherspoon, where the Japanese lay groaning and picking at the bloody scraps of cloth that hung from his knee. It seemed to Witherspoon that Rossi was counting the drops of blood that fell from Harada's groping hand.

"You goddamn gooks," Rossi said after a long silence. "I should have shot the two of you."

Nine

WITHERSPOON was sitting on the floor, shuffling through the papers he had recovered from the cave. His dictionaries were piled on the floor before him, almost as if he had tried to erect a barrier to protect himself from the others in the room. He looked up now and then, but he seemed ill at ease and anxious to make himself as unobtrusive as possible. Across the room, Swenson appeared to be absorbed in picking the broken skin from a dried-up blister on his hand. His back was toward the window where a poncho hung to keep out the driving rain that beat on the roof like tiny pebbles. Rossi was scowling at Swenson, but the sergeant, seemingly oblivious, went on detaching fragments of dead skin from his hand, whistling reedily to himself. Rossi and Witherspoon were wearing clean dungarees — Witherspoon an outsize suit belonging to the doctor — but in spite of their clean clothing and the wind that blew the poncho away from the window the smell of the cave was still in the air.

The doctor came from his own room, carrying a white enamel can full of the sour punch he mixed from his Japanese rum and synthetic lemon powder. He poured the liquid into canteen cups and offered a drink to the others. Witherspoon demurred.

"I don't know if I'd better. My stomach feels a bit queasy."

"Go on," the doctor said. "It'll do you good. If you can get down the first swallow you'll be all right. You need something to calm you down; you're jumpy as a cat." Witherspoon took the drink without any further protest.

"All right," Rossi said suddenly, "let's have the straight poop, Charley. How'd you catch them?"

Swenson was suddenly all business. He forgot about his blister and stopped whistling. "They were up in the gully behind the trees. They tried to run for it when they heard me coming, but I headed them off before they got to the wire. The women didn't even try to get away. They were having a smoke when I brought Fischer and Tucci back."

"Friends of yours?"

"Who — those meatheads Fischer and Tucci?"

"No, the women," Rossi said.

"Never saw them before in my life. A couple of ugly bitches."

Witherspoon had forgotten about his documents and was listening intently to the conversation, astonishment showing on his face. He opened his mouth to speak but thought better of it.

"I thought you had this place organized," Rossi continued. "The way I got it, you'd found yourself a cathouse up in the boondocks at the other end of the stockade. From the racket you were making the other night, I thought you had half the platoon up there."

Swenson blinked. "I guess I got sort of wound up. I had a skinful of this gook liquor."

"You were wound up all right. Tight as an eight-day clock. But what the hell happened, Charley — were you holding out on Fischer and Tucci?"

"They were going to get theirs," Swenson said. "I didn't think those two goof-offs had the guts to try to get it on their own. I don't know what the hell got into them."

"Well, I'll tell you," Rossi said. He drank a big gulp and set his canteen cup on the floor. "You've been hanging around these gooks too long, Charley. When we came down here, I gave you the word — no screwing around. I knew damn well you'd fix something up for yourself but I didn't want to hear about it. I thought you'd have sense enough to keep it quiet. You're getting sloppy, Charley. I'm not interested in what happens to you, but I'm damned if I'm going to let you wreck my platoon. The men have gotten so slack we couldn't win a pillow fight."

"I guess you're right, Lieutenant," Swenson said unhappily. "We're all getting a little rock-happy."

"Tighten things up, Charley. The next time anything happens, there's going to be a new pfc around here. We're playing things by the book from now on."

"Okay, Lieutenant," Swenson lighted a cigarette and puffed on it reflectively.

The doctor went to the window and drew aside the poncho. A sudden blast of wind drove the rain at him and he quietly let the poncho fall back into place.

"I wonder how the people in the stockade make out on a night like this?" he asked. Nobody answered him and he came back into the center of the room. Witherspoon nursed his drink in silence, avoiding any action that would draw Rossi's attention to him. Rossi was staring at the floor.

"These goddamn gooks," Rossi said violently. "Why the hell did we have to get mixed up with them anyway?"

The doctor sat on the floor by Witherspoon. "How do you feel now?"

Witherspoon nodded and attempted a mild joke. "Just what the doctor ordered."

The doctor smiled. "Better let it go with that one, though."

Swenson stirred on his seat by the window. "What happened

with the gook you brought in all shot up? I heard he got away from you. Someone said he would have gotten clean away if it hadn't been for the driver from Division."

"That's right," Rossi said shortly. "He got away from us in the cave."

"Seems funny to me," Swenson said with elaborate casualness. "I never figured a prisoner would get away from you, Lieutenant."

"That's none of your damned business."

"I was just wondering," Swenson said. "It sure seemed funny."

Rossi said nothing for a while. "Shove off, Charley," he said at last. "I've sure had enough of your crap for tonight."

Swenson emptied his drink.

"Go on," Rossi urged. "Get moving. You're going to make me mad."

Swenson picked up his poncho from where it was lying on the floor and pulled it over his head. He took his time in snapping the fasteners on either side. He clapped his helmet on his head and stood in the doorway, looking out into the night.

"It's coming down harder than ever," he observed.

"Get going," Rossi said. Swenson made his way out into the rain.

Rossi extended his empty cup to the doctor. The doctor poured the dregs from the enamel can into Rossi's cup and went into his room for another bottle. Witherspoon, left alone in the room with Rossi, busied himself with his papers, opening his dictionary and turning its pages.

"You'd better put that stuff away," the doctor said, coming back with the rum bottle. "You'll ruin your eyes trying to read in that light."

Witherspoon pushed the papers away, gratefully, as if he had been waiting for just this suggestion. "It's pretty interesting. I think it's just what the colonel wanted."

"Christ, I hope so," Rossi said.

Witherspoon, abashed, toyed with his papers. They were limp with the dampness of the air and exuded an odor of corruption. The doctor finished mixing his punch and filled the empty cups.

"I've been meaning to ask you how you learned Japanese," the doctor said to Witherspoon. "I've learned to speak a bit of it, but I understand it's a pretty tough language to read — thousands of characters and so forth."

"Anybody can learn it if they work at it long enough," Witherspoon said modestly. "It doesn't take any particular talent to memorize characters."

"It's certainly a remarkable accomplishment," the doctor said sententiously. "If I were twenty years younger, I'd like to have a crack at it myself. I was pretty good at French in college."

"Seems a damn silly way to write," Rossi said. "What did you do, Witherspoon, spend a couple of years learning to draw pictures?"

"Now, now," the doctor intervened, "we can't all understand what the other fellow's interested in."

"How come you got into the marines?" Rossi asked. "You don't look like a marine type to me."

"I volunteered," Witherspoon said self-consciously.

"It must have been a great day for the marines," Rossi said. His cup was empty again and he pushed it across the floor to the doctor.

The doctor obliged, but with reluctance. "Take it easy; this stuff sneaks up on you."

"I think I can handle it," Rossi said.

"All right, all right, I didn't say you couldn't," the doctor said hurriedly.

The poncho at the window flapped again in the wind and a gust of rain blew inside the room. There was a crashing sound from within the stockade, followed by a burst of shouting.

"Somebody's roof must have blown off," the doctor said. "Maybe I'd better have a look at sick bay."

"I wouldn't worry about it," Rossi said. "Sick bay's anchored down pretty securely. If anything blows apart, the gooks can take care of it."

Nevertheless the doctor plodded into his room and returned wrapped in a poncho. A helmet-liner was perched on his head. When he lifted his arms, the folds of the poncho flapped like the wings of an ungainly bird. "I'll be back in a few minutes, I'm just going to check up on a couple of things."

There was a silence after the doctor had left. Rossi got up and took down the pistol belt that was hanging from a nail on the wall. "Hell, I forgot all about your pistol. I suppose you want it back."

"Thanks." Witherspoon watched Rossi field strip the pistol and prepare to clean out the bore. "You don't need to do that," Witherspoon said, but Rossi went on cleaning the weapon.

"I'm sorry as hell for the way I blew up in the cave," Witherspoon said. "I acted pretty badly, I guess."

"You sure did," Rossi said, without looking up from his work. "You couldn't have acted much worse."

"It was the first time I was mixed up in anything like that. I guess I just lost my head."

"They didn't have any business sending you down here in the first place. You'd better stay close to Division after this."

Witherspoon flushed. "I think it'll be better the next time."

108

"Well," Rossi said, "maybe it will, but I hope I'm not around." He squinted down the barrel of the pistol and, satisfied with what he saw, began to assemble the parts.

The conversation threatened to lag and Witherspoon hastened to fill the gap. "How many prisoners do you have in this stockade?"

"We've never counted them," Rossi said, amiably enough. Either the liquor or Witherspoon's apology had blunted the fine edge of his anger. "There were about five thousand when we came. We've gotten some new ones in but they just about balance out the ones that've died. I figure it's about the same — five thousand, more or less."

"That seems a lot for one platoon."

"It's a good handful. We're understrength as hell anyway."

"It must be quite a job."

"I can keep them from breaking out and I can keep them from starving to death but I can't keep them from raising hell with my men. When I first came here, the doctor was running around like a chicken with its head cut off. We got the place organized, but as soon as we did, the gooks began working on my men." He slipped the pistol back into its holster before he went on. "They're cagey little bastards. Take Fischer: He's a good rifle-man but he's as stupid as they come. If you can't keep him busy all day long he's bound to get in trouble. The gooks have liquor and women. Fischer's always thirsty and he likes a quick piece of tail as well as the next man. It's Swenson's job to keep Fischer in line. Well, Swenson goofed off. Now I'm stuck with a platoon of marines I don't trust and five thousand gooks, every one of them itching to see me get knocked off. I was out there when they were lining up for chow the other night. I watched them come up to get their rice and after each one I said to myself,

'Rossi, that bastard is out to get you, but you're going to get him first.' "

"I don't think it can be as bad as that," Witherspoon said. "They looked pretty harmless to me."

"Oh, they're not going to start a revolution. That isn't what worries me." Rossi drank slowly from his cup. "It's too bad you haven't seen the looney bin. You'll probably hear it later tonight."

"Hear what?" Witherspoon asked.

"We have some lunatics we keep in a cage up on the mountain. There's a crazy geisha up there. She'll probably begin singing as soon as the rain lets up. It's not loud, but it wakes me up every time. I lie here on this sack and I listen to her howling and I wonder how long it's going to take the gooks to get me." He got up from the cot and moved around the room restlessly, stopping at the window to draw aside the poncho. The rain blew in and dampened him but he remained there for a moment, sniffing at the air as if it might tell him what was going on inside the stockade.

"Those goddamn gooks," he said. "I'm going to take a look inside. You want to come along?"

"It's raining," Witherspoon objected.

"Stay here if you like," Rossi said. "I don't give a damn."

The guard at the gate crouched miserably in the meager protection afforded by a scraggly pine. A steady stream of water trickled from the edge of his helmet onto his soggy poncho. He lifted his head when he heard Rossi and Witherspoon approach and Rossi's flashlight illuminated a boy's wet face.

"Don't take it so hard," Rossi said. "Your relief's going to have it worse than you do."

The boy grinned unhappily.

"I'm going to show this officer around the stockade," Rossi told him. "If the doctor comes out, tell him where we are."

The boy opened the gate and the light swung away and they left him hunched up in the stormy night. Witherspoon followed Rossi through the mud of the square to a shed that sheltered a row of huge iron kettles. It was dry under the shed, but water had collected in pools under the kettles. Witherspoon was already beginning to sweat under the rubberized poncho.

"What do you want to see first?" Rossi asked. "Take you anywhere you want."

Witherspoon observed that he'd just come along for the ride.

"Come on, then," Rossi said and struck out across the square.

As soon as they had left the protection of the shed Witherspoon began to regret his decision to accompany Rossi. The comforting effect of the doctor's rum had already worn off and left him weak and aching where he had bruised himself in the cave. His breathing was strained and his heart pumped too rapidly. But Rossi drove ahead, undeterred by the clayey mud and the steady beat of the rain on his face. They left the square and started along a trail through the trees.

"The gooks are all in their houses tonight," Rossi pointed out.

He flashed the light to the side of the trail and Witherspoon saw a group of small huts, dark and silent in the rain. They continued on the trail and their only encounter was with a spotted dog that yapped at their heels.

Their journey seemed to Witherspoon to be interminable. He had developed a limp, which was aggravated by his continual slipping in the mud. But Rossi went on, turning off onto another trail and then another, always going deeper into the maze of paths among the huts where the prisoners lived. They came suddenly on an old man walking barefoot in the rain. The old man stood for an instant in the beam of the light and then turned and fled.

It was five minutes later, when Witherspoon, utterly exhausted, was on the point of begging Rossi to return, that they saw a light through the trees. Rossi flicked off the switch of his light and made his way in the dark, Witherspoon close behind him, to a hut where the light of a candle shone from a window. When they were close enough to see what was going on inside, Rossi put out an arm to stop Witherspoon, and the two men stood motionless in the rain and watched the scene inside the window.

A woman was combing her long hair by the light of the candle. She was naked to the waist and the smooth skin of her body glowed in the light, a rich, creamy color in contrast to her black hair. She bowed her head and combed the dark mass of her hair forward over her face until the long heavy strands fell over her breasts. A girl appeared and sat on the floor and spoke with the woman. The woman laughed huskily but went on combing out her hair. She spoke wheedlingly and the girl sat behind her and began to massage her back, kneading the smooth, firm muscles of her neck and shoulders. The woman stopped combing her hair, abandoning herself to the pleasure of the girl's hands on her back. In a little while she shook herself and the girl desisted.

"It's the goddamn Madame," Rossi muttered.

"What?" Witherspoon had forgotten his aching knee and if his breathing was still quick and irregular, he knew it was not the long walk that was entirely to blame.

"Come on," Rossi said, starting forward toward the house.

The Madame heard them coming and, taking sudden alarm,

shook the hair from her face and drew the kimono around her shoulders. But when Rossi was at the door and she saw who her visitor was she let it fall again to the floor and with a few rapid strokes of her comb drew her hair back from her face so that it fell smooth and glossy over her shoulders.

She smiled and inclined her head and said something to Rossi.

"What's that?" Rossi demanded.

"She says to please come in. She's sorry she isn't ready for you but she didn't know you were coming."

The girl who had massaged the Madame's back and another girl began to scurry around the room, tidying up; they smiled at their guests.

"You want to go in?" Rossi asked.

Witherspoon was silent, not trusting himself to answer. The dry cheerful room, the amiable girls, and most of all, the half-naked figure of the Madame, inviting them in with a smile, were almost too much for him to bear.

"You know," Rossi said in a strained voice, "that's the only gook woman I've seen out here that I wouldn't kick out of bed."

The Madame urged them to enter, coming to the doorway. "Come," she said to Witherspoon, "nobody will see you. Come in and have some hot tea." She leaned forward and tugged lightly at Witherspoon's poncho. He recoiled from her bare skin as if he had touched something hot and burning.

Rossi looked down at the woman who was kneeling in front of him, looking up at him with disbelief at his reluctance. "Tell her that I'm not coming in tonight or any other night. Neither is anybody else. Swenson's had his last party. From now on, she'd better find some other way to amuse herself at night."

Witherspoon translated as best he could and followed Rossi out of the shelter of the hut and into the rain. At the bend of the trail he stopped and looked back. The Madame was still in the doorway, her bare body silhouetted in the light of the candle.

Even now Rossi was not satisfied with his inspection of the camp; he led the way through the narrow paths between the huts, and Witherspoon, stupid from fatigue, slipped and stumbled alongside him, afraid more than anything else of being left alone without a light in the rabbit warren of the stockade. They began to climb, and Rossi led Witherspoon up a narrow trail that finally brought them out on a flat shelf of land.

Rossi swung the beam of his flashlight onto a cage of wire, one end of which was covered with a tarpaulin. Rossi let the light linger only long enough for Witherspoon to make out a cluster of bodies huddled on the ground under the canvas.

"What's that?"

"The nuts," Rossi said. He went no nearer to the cage but veered off toward where the shelf fell off into a wilderness of tangled brush. Below them in the distance they could see lights in Swenson's hut and in the long, barrackslike shed behind, where the main body of the men lived. To the right, there was a single light that might have come from the Madame's house. Otherwise there was only a vast expanse of darkness where the prisoners huddled in the meager huts that kept them from the rain.

There was an angry chattering from behind them that made Witherspoon jump and cry out. Rossi turned his light on the cage. A ragged figure stood inside the wire, oblivious to the rain that beat on his face and washed his emaciated body. In his hand he held an empty tin can that he stretched out supplicatingly toward the two marines.

"It's only Smoky Joe wanting a drink of water," Rossi said. He switched the light off and left Smoky Joe crying in the dark.

Witherspoon leaned for support against a tree that hung over the declivity below them. His helmet had become intolerably heavy and he took it off and let the rain strike his bare head. Underneath the poncho his body, suffocated in the airless pouch, was running with sweat. His mind was filled with a fantastic jumble of images: the row of corpses at the entrance to the cave, the Madame's naked breasts, Swenson calmly peeling the dead skin from his hand, and the wretched figure of the lunatic who was still chattering in the cage behind him.

"You've seen it now," he heard Rossi say. "What do you make of it?"

Witherspoon attempted to apply his mind to the question, but the only answer of which he was certain was that he wanted to be rid of the stockade as quickly as possible. "I don't know," he said. "I don't know what to make of it."

"You ought to stay around," Rossi said and his voice was hard and confident. "I'm going to lower the boom on these bastards, the gooks and the others. In a week this place is going to be so tight that if anyone goofs off long enough to scratch his ass, I'm going to know about it. They're going to sweat, Witherspoon. I'm going to see to it that they sweat like hell. You don't think I can do it, do you?"

"I don't know," Witherspoon said. "I don't even know what you're talking about."

Rossi flashed the light in Witherspoon's face. "Christ, you look like hell. Let's get out of here."

Witherspoon gratefully fell in behind him as Rossi showed the way down through the stockade to his hut.

Ten

WHEN Swenson awoke the sun was shining through the mosquito net onto his face and onto the smooth brown back of the girl who lay pressed against him on the narrow cot. Swenson lay there for a moment, blinking in the sunlight and absently stroking the girl's arm; then he shot out of bed and fumbled on the ground for his shoes. Mike, who was sleeping in the second of the three beds, rolled over and covered his eyes with his arm. Taliaferro's bed was empty.

"Je-sus Kee-rist," Swenson muttered. "Jesus Christ on a crutch! Wake up, Peggy, wake up, damn it!" He shook the girl roughly. She rolled onto her back and lay placidly in the sunlight, her eyes screwed up against the moment of waking. When Swenson shook her again she opened her eyes and smiled sleepily.

"Wake up," Swenson whispered hoarsely, "chop-chop!"

The girl shook herself and rolled out of bed, suddenly wide awake and frightened.

"Get away from that window!" Swenson ordered, pushing the girl toward the wall. He tossed her thin cotton dress to her and began to pull on his dungarees. When the girl was dressed, Swenson led her to the rear of the hut. He helped her wriggle through the narrow window and leaned out after her.

"Run! Chop-chop!"

She ran like a frightened rabbit to the gate. Taliaferro who was sitting at the gate talking to the guard, sprang to his feet and began to wrestle with the bolt. He swung the gate halfway open and Swenson saw the girl dart safely into the stockade.

Swenson finished dressing and strolled casually toward Rossi's hut. Rossi was sleeping heavily. His mosquito net had come undone and one of his legs extended from under the net and hung loosely from the side of the cot. The mosquitoes had been at work on his leg, but Rossi slept on undisturbed.

Swenson walked rapidly to the gate. Taliaferro had resumed his conversation with the guard as if nothing had happened.

"You son of a bitch!" Swenson said.

Taliaferro looked up innocently.

"You would have screwed things up fine if the lieutenant had caught me with that girl."

"What girl? I haven't seen any girl."

"You know goddamn well what girl."

"Oh, *that* girl."

"Don't get wise, Mac," Swenson said savagely.

"I know, Charley," Taliaferro said placatingly. "I forgot. I damn near pissed in my pants when she came shooting out of the hut."

"You forgot! Christ on a crutch!"

"I'm sorry, Charley, honest to God."

"Ah, you stupid son of a bitch, Taliaferro." Swenson turned on his heel and went back to his quarters, brooding over his narrow escape. The cooks had risen and were at work preparing breakfast in the galley at the end of the long barracks, but Swenson set about making his usual prebreakfast coffee. He brewed it in a large tin can over a can of sterno. When it was hot and bubbling he threw in a handful of sugar cubes to give it body and called Mike, who came to the door, wearing only his skivvies. Mike sat in the doorway and blinked in the sunlight, scratching his lean body into wakefulness. Swenson poured out two cups of coffee and the two men sat on the doorsill in the sunlight, blowing on their coffee and watching the front of Rossi's hut.

"That goof-off Taliaferro," Swenson said. "He was supposed to wake us up before sunrise."

Mike sucked in his coffee loudly. "Seems to me you're taking one hell of a chance. The way that girl was squealing last night, you're going to have the lieutenant on our necks before long."

Swenson smiled. "Peggy's a good kid. I think she likes me. Reminds me of a little happahaole girl I was shacked up with on Maui. I wouldn't of brought her here only it was raining so hard I figured the lieutenant wouldn't hear anything. He was drinking with the doctor and that lieutenant from Division."

"I don't like it," Mike said. "The lieutenant was plenty mad yesterday. Maybe we can get away with it, but maybe he's going to land on us like a ton of bricks. It's not smart to take any chances, not after you turned in Fischer and Tucci."

"I got that squared with him. He ate my ass out a bit last night and that ought to keep him happy for a while. As long as we keep out of his way, he's not going to make any trouble. Hell, Mike, Rossi and I've been together for almost three years now; we understand each other."

"What happened to Fischer and Tucci?"

"They'll be working their asses off for a while. Rossi's not out for blood yet."

"I don't care if he's out for blood or not, I don't want that son of a bitch working my ass off. He doesn't like me."

"He doesn't have anything against you. He just doesn't like gooks."

"That doesn't make much difference to me," Mike said. "I don't care why he doesn't like me; I just don't want him on my back."

"I'll take care of that." Swenson sipped his coffee thoughtfully. "I was wondering, Mike, what's your angle on this?"

"Angle on what?"

"After all, you're a Jap yourself. I was wondering how I'd feel if it was the Swedes we were fighting. My folks always talked Swedish at home."

"I've already told you I came out here to kill Japs," Mike said, as if that were a sufficient answer. "I don't like Japs."

"I know," Swenson said, "but what I was wondering about is why you don't like Japs."

"Look, Charley, do you like Japs?"

"I hate the little yellow bastards," Swenson said promptly.

"So do I," Mike said.

Swenson waved his cup toward the stockade where the sounds of the morning were becoming audible. "What about them?"

"Those people are all right. They just got taken for a ride. It's the Japs I don't like."

Swenson was about to press the point when it occurred to him that his girl Peggy was certainly a gook and possibly a Jap. He mused silently over this paradox.

Loomis emerged from his shack at the corner of the compound and stretched in the sunlight. He washed his face in a helmet full of rain water and then came over to where Swenson and Mike were sitting.

"How about some coffee?"

Swenson pointed to the can, which was still more than half

full, and Loomis stooped over and filled his cup. He remained standing, looking down on the other two. Loomis carried an air of foreboding around with him like a bad smell.

"Looks like there's going to be some changes around here."

"What do you mean?" Swenson asked cautiously.

"I heard the lieutenant sounding off last night. Sounded like he'd caught up with you."

"The lieutenant and I get along all right. You take care of sick bay and I'll take care of the lieutenant."

"Which one of the girls did you have?"

"What's it to you?"

Loomis shrugged. "If you want to get a dose, it's no skin off my ass."

"This girl's all right," Swenson said.

"I wouldn't be so sure. Was it the plump little girl I've seen you with? She doesn't look very healthy to me."

"You're a mean son of a bitch," Swenson said.

The argument lapsed into a hostile silence.

The doctor was next to arrive. He buttoned his chest into a too-tight shirt as he came, fumbling for the buttonholes. The lieutenant from Division straggled after him, looking pale and tired in the bright morning light. Swenson poured two more cups and offered his seat to the doctor. The strange lieutenant nursed his coffee a little apart.

"Say, Doc, this character's trying to tell me my little gook girl ain't healthy."

"I think she's all right," the doctor said. "Probably the worst you'll get is a case of crabs. *Pes pediculos*. That means little pattering feet in private places."

Loomis wasn't amused. "You can't tell. She may be infectious as hell."

"No, I can't tell for sure, but I think she's all right."

"This is a hell of a time to tell me," Swenson complained.

"What about me?" Mike broke in to ask. "Nobody seems to worry about me."

"I think you'll live," the doctor said. "If either of you notice any symptoms, come up and see me right away."

"I'll take care of you myself," Loomis offered. "You'll love every minute of it."

"Ah, shut up. I don't like you Loomis. You're one of the meanest bastards I've ever known. If I cut my finger I wouldn't let you put a band-aid on it."

"The offer's still open."

"Where's the lieutenant?" Swenson asked the doctor. "He's usually out of the sack by now. I've been saving a cup of coffee for him."

"I think he's going to be a little late," the doctor said. "He and Lieutenant Witherspoon were wandering around the stockade until all hours last night. When they came back they finished up my last bottle, damn it."

Lieutenant Witherspoon smiled wanly. He was listening to the conversation but seemed inclined to keep his own counsel.

"I can get you some more," Swenson said. "We're really going to get into production this week."

The doctor nodded but he looked worried. "I'd watch that stuff if I were you, Charley. You don't want to overdo a good thing."

"That's what I've been telling him," Mike said.

"I've been careless," Swenson admitted. "But everything's under control now. I don't think the lieutenant's going to see anything he oughtn't to."

The doctor swirled the dregs of his coffee to stir up the sugar at the bottom of the cup. "I wish I knew exactly what you're up to, Charley. You're going to get your ass in a sling one of these days."

"Well, if you don't know, you can't do anything about it."

"It might be better if I could. The way things look to me, the lieutenant may pull the rug out from under you when you're not expecting it."

"I'll keep things under control," Swenson promised.

The doctor stood up heavily. "Come on, Loomis." He set off briskly for the gate, followed by Loomis.

Lieutenant Witherspoon put down his cup, still partly full of coffee, and spoke for the first time. "Do you know where my driver is?"

"Sure. Do you want him now?"

"Yes. We have to get back to the C.P."

"Mike'll get him for you."

Mike pulled on his shoes and went to the shed. Swenson and the lieutenant waited for Corcoran in front of the hut.

"How do you like the setup we've got here?" Swenson asked. "It's probably a lot different up at Division."

"It is," Lieutenant Witherspoon said. Swenson didn't know if the lieutenant was short-spoken because of natural surliness or because of his share of the doctor's last bottle of liquor, so he let the conversation drop. He was taking a jeep down the road to try to scrounge some more wire and he waited impatiently for Mike to return and get the lieutenant on his way.

Rossi was waiting at the gate when the working party of women returned from the warehouse down the road with the day's supply of rice. The procession of women, each with a

122

straw sack on her shoulder, was led by Kaneshiro and guarded by Mike and Davis. The women carried the heavy sacks easily, at a pace between a walk and a trot. They arrived at the gate with only a slight beading of sweat on their upper lips to show their exertion. Rossi watched them trot through the open gate into the square. When all but the last two women were inside, he called to the guard to close the gate. The two women stood dumbly balancing their burdens.

"Take them back, Davis," Rossi said. He motioned to Mike. "You stay with me."

Kaneshiro came forward, his face creased in an ingratiating smile. "Sergeant Swenson say okay. Rice for hospital." He ordered the women to lower their sacks to the ground and displayed the contents to Rossi. One of the sacks was full of rice; the other contained canned Japanese army rations. Kaneshiro took two cans from the second sack and showed them to Rossi. "Beef. Fish. Very good for sick person."

"You're lying," Rossi said coldly. "This is the last time you're going to leave the stockade. Get them moving, Davis." The two women wheeled around and trotted stolidly back toward the warehouse, shepherded by Davis.

Rossi passed through the gate, followed by Mike and Kaneshiro. The cooks had fallen to work at the galley. They broke open the sacks of rice and poured the rice into their kettles, to be washed, boiled, and ladled out to the prisoners. Rossi and a host of children watched them at their work.

"Let's go see the still," Rossi said.

Mike hesitated. "What do you mean, the still?"

"You know the way," Rossi said. "Let's not waste any time playing dumb."

Kaneshiro was suddenly reminded of urgent business elsewhere. "Come back here," Rossi ordered. "I'm going to need you too."

The dew was still on the bushes that screened the gulley from the path and Rossi's dungarees were spotted with water when he broke through the underbrush into the clearing where Gushiken was tending his two stills. Gushiken was feeding the fire under the larger still and didn't see his visitors for a moment. When he looked up he saw Kaneshiro's distressed countenance and moved aside, uncertain as to Rossi's purpose. Rossi sniffed the air, sour with the smell of mash and the warm, fresh liquor.

Rossi motioned to Kaneshiro and pointed to the wooden tubs of mash. "Start dumping it."

Kaneshiro bent over unhappily and lifted one side of a tub, while Gushiken stood stock still, stricken with inarticulate horror. Kaneshiro groaned under the weight of the tub, struggling with its weight until he had lifted it to the vertical. The mash flowed around him in an irregularly shaped pool that drained away, leaving a thick scum on the surface of the ground.

"Turn it over."

Kaneshiro let the tub fall to the ground, top uppermost.

"Get on top and jump on it."

Kaneshiro obeyed. The tub collapsed with a splintering crash. Gushiken was ordered to dispose of the second tub in the same way. He began to obey, but suddenly dropped the tub with a strangled cry and streaked for the bushes. He was heard for a while as he floundered through the underbrush.

"I guess you'll have to finish it alone," Rossi said.

Kaneshiro destroyed the second tub. When he was through, he was set to dismantling the two stills. Rossi took the coils of copper tubing, still hot to the touch. At last there was left a mound of splintered wood, the shards of earthenware jugs, and two open kettles. The only liquor that was left was the mash that still steamed in the larger kettle, dissipating its alcoholic fumes into the morning air.

They walked back to the square in silence. Kaneshiro's face was set in an expression of long-suffering martyrdom.

"How much have you and Charley been getting from them?" Rossi asked Mike.

"About a bottle a day. We haven't been drinking it all ourselves though. Charley's been rationing it out to the other men."

Kaneshiro was still trailing them obediently. "That's all for you," Rossi said. "I don't want to see you again."

Kaneshiro stood his ground. "Go on. Get out of my sight."

Kaneshiro waved and broke. "Okay," he said. "Okay, I see." He padded off with as much dignity as he could muster.

The cooks had begun to serve the morning meal and Rossi stood under the shed with them and watched the distribution of the rice. The prisoners' customarily lively mealtime chatter was subdued; they watched Rossi warily as they approached the head of the line and when they had received their portion of rice they hurried away as if they were afraid that Rossi would snatch the food from their hands.

"Let's move on," Rossi said. He led the way toward sick bay and Mike followed.

"You seem to get along real well with the gooks," Rossi said. "It seems funny to me that we didn't have any trouble until you came down here."

"I didn't ask to be sent to your platoon," Mike reminded him. "This liquor and stuff wasn't my idea."

"Well, Swenson wouldn't have gotten so many ideas himself if you hadn't been around to do the talking for him. You ought to be glad you're in the army. If you were a marine, I'd have you broken so quickly you wouldn't know what had hit you."

"I'll be damned glad to get back to the army, Lieutenant," Mike said earnestly. "Nobody in the army treated me like a Jap spy."

The shuttered walls had been drawn aside for the day and the patients in the ward were grumbling peevishly over fancied inequalities in the bowls of rice brought them by the squinty nurse. Rossi stopped and looked again at a man who lay motionless on his pallet, paying no heed to the nurse when she offered him a bowl of rice. His face was a liverish green and he stared listlessly at the ceiling with feverish eyes.

"Where've I seen that gook before?" Rossi demanded.

"He's Harada," Mike said. "The man we took to the cave."

"That son of a bitch," Rossi said.

Harada turned his head and stared uncomprehendingly at Rossi.

"You goddamned son of a bitch," Rossi said with feeling. The doctor had heard him and came from the dressing room, a roll of gauze in his hand.

"Leave my patients alone," he ordered. "You almost killed that man the other day. Isn't that enough?"

The doctor went back to the dressing room and went on with his work. He stripped a greasy bandage from an old woman's hand and swabbed the deep suppurating wound underneath. The old woman cried out once, an anguished, quickly suppressed moan. The doctor applied a fresh dressing and turned to a boy whose face was broken out in festering ulcers.

"Business is getting slack," the doctor said, "but I still manage to keep busy."

"Been having any trouble up here?" Rossi asked.

"Trouble? My only trouble is getting these people to show up for treatment. They don't like doctors. They don't usually come to me until a couple of days later than they ought to. Why do you want to know?"

"We're going to tighten things up around here," Rossi said. "There's been too much funny business going on in this stockade."

"I'm inclined to agree with you," the doctor said, "but this is a sick bay and I'm a doctor and I'd just as soon you left this place to me. Unless you're sick, you don't have any more business here than I would if I tried to take over your platoon for you."

"It seems to me we've both gotten mixed up in each other's business. Somehow, I have the idea you know more about some of the things that have been going on than I do."

"I haven't gone out of my way to find out anything. I learned long ago to keep my mouth shut when people told me things I had no business knowing."

"I'm glad to find out where you stand," Rossi said. "It looks like I'm going to have to clean up this place alone."

The doctor paused in his ministrations to the boy with the yaws. "Now look here," he said, his voice strained with sudden anger, "you gave me a song and dance the other day about how all you needed to do was to lift your hand and everything would fall into place. You've let things get into one hell of a mess and I'd be willing to bet that things are going to get worse before they get any better. If you're serious about cleaning this place up, I'm willing to do anything I can to help, but I'll be goddamned if I'm going to take any nonsense from you about my part in this. If you don't like the way I run sick bay that's just too bad; I don't like the way you run the stockade."

Rossi didn't answer immediately. The doctor's anger subsided as he waited for Rossi to speak, leaving him looking sheepish at his outburst. Of the two other men, Loomis appeared to be absorbed in treating a patient, and Mike masked his interest under an impassive Oriental exterior.

"All right," Rossi said, "if you're so anxious to help, maybe you can tell me a few things I want to know. Where's Swenson getting his liquor?"

"I don't know," the doctor said truthfully. "There's a still somewhere in the stockade."

"You'll be happy to know we already found it. We smashed it. I have another question. Where does Swenson get his women?"

Loomis spoke up. "Why don't you ask Mike? He could probably take you there blindfolded."

Mike waited stolidly for the onslaught he expected but Rossi paid no attention to him.

"It doesn't look to me," Rossi said, "as if you're going to be much use anyway. All you seem to be good for is taking care of sick bay."

"That's all I've ever wanted," the doctor said wearily. "You can run the stockade any way you want, but for God's sake let me handle things up here my own way."

Three of the Madame's girls — Peggy, Judy, and a thickset girl with a cast in one eye — were on their hands and knees, scrubbing the floor with water and sand. Outside, the Madame herself watched a pot in which clothing was boiling. She sang to herself in a low voice and now and again stirred the pot with a wooden paddle. She continued to sing even after she heard someone coming up the path. When Rossi and Mike turned off the path into the yard in front of the house, she looked up, genuinely startled.

She greeted them politely and apologized for the disorder in which her visitors had surprised her. Neither of the men acknowledged her remarks. Rossi went to the door and looked inside. The girls stopped their work and gawked at him. The Madame offered him a seat on the floor where the water had already dried and left the wood clean and fresh. Rossi shook his head and remained standing. The Madame spoke sharply to the girls and sent them back to work.

The Madame talked to Mike at some length.

"What's she saying?" Rossi broke in.

Mike looked at him and translated the Madame's speech flatly, as if he had no conception of the meaning of the words.

"She wonders why you didn't stay longer last night. She wonders if you know that she operated the entertainment house for the Japanese staff officers. She says she once entertained General Matsui personally. He was a handsome man and kind to her but he was old, not young and vigorous like you."

"Tell her I saw General Matsui recently," Rossi said. "He was dead as a doornail."

The Madame bowed her head for a moment but when she lifted it her eyes were bright and eager.

"She says that in that case she will be all the happier to have you visit her."

Rossi took his time. He lighted a cigarette and inspected the Madame critically. "You know, you and Swenson didn't do badly at all. Which one of you had the Madame?"

"Neither of us," Mike said. "She says she always saves herself for the commanding officer."

Rossi waited a moment longer before he spoke. "Tell her the party's over. She's not going to get any visits from the commanding officer or anyone else. If I catch her or any of the girls so much as looking at one of the men she's going to peddle her business from inside the loony cage."

The Madame bowed her head to indicate that she had understood.

Rossi and Mike were halfway back to the square when Mike spoke up. "Did the Madame say you were at her house last night, Lieutenant?"

"It's none of your goddamn business," Rossi said savagely. "What's more, I'm going to break your yellow neck for you if you say anything about it again."

Eleven

LIEUTENANT-COLONEL Smith, the Division intelligence officer, was a small man, just a fraction of an inch over the minimum height required for officers of the Marine Corps. In his eighteen years of service he had, by dint of diligent self-control, cultivated a hard-bitten look he had hoped would cause his brother officers to forget his Academy nickname, Peanut. The outthrust jaw and the thin, snapping-turtle mouth had become as much a part of him as his bristling crew cut, but in moments when he was unobserved, the sternness disappeared from his eyes and left him looking like a bemused professor. It was in this mood that he sat at the field desk in his tent and watched Corporal Chernik working on the situation map. Chernik was entering reports of enemy patrols on the acetate overlay. There were fewer entries to make each day as a skirmish line of marines moved south over territory they had once already fought over.

The sternness came back to the colonel's eyes when he heard a jeep pull up outside. He saw Witherspoon, his youngest and newest officer, climb out of the jeep and head for the door of the tent. The colonel was reminded of a remark of Captain Fishman's. The only thing he didn't like about Witherspoon, Fishman had said, was that he always looked so goddamned bewildered. The bewildered look was still there, the colonel observed, and he wondered if he would ever succeed in educating Witherspoon at least to look the part he was supposed to be playing. The colonel understandably placed considerable weight on this achievement.

"Well, Witherspoon," the colonel barked as soon as the language officer was inside the tent, "what sort of luck did you have?"

"We found the general, sir," Witherspoon said. He laid a large packet of papers on Smith's desk. "These are the documents I picked up."

The colonel's snapping-turtle mask almost broke into a smile but he had control of himself before Witherspoon was aware of more than a momentary relaxation of the muscles around his mouth. "Did he shoot himself or commit hara-kiri?"

"Poison," Witherspoon said.

"By God," the colonel snapped, "I would have thought the old boy had more guts than that." He looked sharply at Witherspoon and was annoyed to see that the look of bewilderment seemed to have increased rather than diminished. "You look as if you'd had a rough time."

"It was pretty bad," Witherspoon said.

"Let's hear about it." The colonel indicated a folding stool and Witherspoon sat down and told him about it. Witherspoon glossed over very little, tempering only his account of his escape from the cave. The story tumbled out of him in a rush and when he was through he fixed his eyes on the wall of the tent above the colonel's head and waited. The colonel was notorious for the precision with which he could lay bare the mental and moral deficiencies of a subordinate.

"You know, Witherspoon, I could have sent down Leventhal

or Kelly." Witherspoon was not deceived by the colonel's conversational tone. "They've both been with me for a couple of operations and they know how to take care of themselves. I decided to send you down and I picked you for a good reason. You're green as hell and I wanted to know how you'd make out. You might have gotten into a firefight and that wouldn't have done you any harm. Provided, of course, you didn't manage to get yourself killed. Now that you know why I sent you, how do you think you made out?"

"Pretty badly," Witherspoon said.

"I'm inclined to agree with you," the colonel said. "If it had been Kelly or Leventhal, I would have given them the goddamnedest chewing out they ever heard. But considering everything, I'm not too disappointed in you. You found out what you were supposed to find out and you brought me back the proof. All right, when the shooting began, you ran like hell. I think everyone's entitled to one bad show. As far as I'm concerned, Witherspoon, you did your job. Nobody's going to know about the rest unless you tell them." His glance shifted to the back of Corporal Chernik, who was still assiduously marking the situation map. "Chernik wouldn't be here if he didn't know how to keep his mouth shut."

Chernik turned around for the first time and grinned. "Hell, Lieutenant, the first time I made a landing, the sergeant had to kick my ass out of the hole I was digging for myself. I was going so fast I would have struck oil in another couple of minutes."

Witherspoon smiled for the first time.

"There's just one more thing," the colonel said. "I said everyone's entitled to one bad show. That doesn't mean two. If anything like this happens the next time, don't let me hear about it."

He shuffled through the papers Witherspoon had brought from the cave, pausing to look closely at a map.

"What did you make of this lieutenant who's running the stockade? Rossi."

"He's sort of a wild man," Witherspoon said. He told the colonel of the nocturnal expedition through the stockade, omitting their visit with the Madame.

"I took him out of George Lannigan's battalion," the colonel said. "His platoon had caught more than their share and George wanted to give them a rest. It sounds to me as if he's had just about enough of the stockade."

"All I know is that he hates the prisoners," Witherspoon said.

"He probably didn't belong up there in the first place," the colonel said. "Anyway, he won't be up there for more than a couple of days. We've finally tracked down this half-witted military government outfit that's supposed to be taking care of the civilians. They are without doubt the most fouled up group of men I have seen anywhere at any time. They've managed to lose half their equipment and they've been sitting on this LST in the bay, howling for help and refusing to come ashore until their C.O. finds out who stole his sleeping bag. Don't ask me what he's going to do with a sleeping bag on this island. We've finally lit a fire under them and I don't think they're going to be able to stall for more than a couple of days longer. Rossi ought to be happy to get out of there."

"I think he will be," Witherspoon said.

"There's another thing I wanted to ask you about. You said that you think this prisoner who took you to the cave was probably a Jap soldier."

"I can't be sure," Witherspoon said. "But I wouldn't be sur-

134

prised. The Nisei boy, Mike, seemed pretty sure he was a soldier."

"He's probably right. I've gotten reports from the collecting points that in the last couple of days they've picked up half a dozen Japs trying to sneak through with the civilians. Some of them didn't even have the sense to throw away their uniforms, just tore off their insignia and tried to mix with the civilians. I think we can assume that the ones we caught were the stupid ones. I wouldn't care to guess how many others got through. At any rate, we're going to have to get them out. Somebody back at Pearl has been screaming his head off that he wants to get all the POW's back as soon as possible. I think I'm going to have to send someone down to the stockade to screen them all and see how many we can yank out of there."

"It would be one hell of a job, Colonel," Witherspoon said.

The colonel grunted. He sprang to his feet and went to the situation map. Chernik moved his stool to the side.

"Come here. I want you to show me where you found the cave."

Witherspoon traced with his finger the road that went down to the west coast of the island, found the escarpment, and the road that they had taken along the rocky coast.

"It was about here. I have it marked on my own map." His fingers had smeared one of the red crayon lines Chernik had been drawing and he absently rubbed the crayon mark with his thumb. He looked at the map again and saw that the line he had smeared had indicated an enemy patrol of fifty men. "Dear God," Witherspoon said softly, "I thought that area had all been cleaned up."

The colonel took Chernik's wax pencil and restored the fifty

Japanese. "That's no reason for you to go messing up our map. What about the other job I gave you? Did you pick up anything for the Old Man?"

"I left it in the jeep. The driver's keeping an eye on it."

Witherspoon followed the colonel through the entrance of the tent to where Corcoran lounged behind the wheel of the jeep. Corcoran had already disposed of the small armory of swords and pistols he himself had picked up and only the general's sword in its plain black scabbard lay in the back seat. Witherspoon handed it to the Colonel. Colonel Smith slipped the sword from its scabbard and held the blade in the sunlight. It was perfect, without a spot of rust or a careless fingerprint to mar the polished steel. He held the blade close to him and pointed out to Witherspoon the thin, wavy line that ran roughly parallel to the cutting edge. Between the line and the edge the steel had a softer polish and seemed to be almost translucent.

"Know what that is?"

"No sir," Witherspoon admitted.

"You're a hell of an intelligence officer," the colonel said. "You'd be in a nasty spot if the Old Man himself asked you about it. There's one thing I want you to remember. Your Japanese may be so bad you couldn't even order yourself a bowl of *soba;* you may not even know the difference between a *rikusentai* and a *boeitai.* Don't let that bother you. You'll get ahead in this game just as long as you can explain souvenirs to the high brass."

His voice was becoming bitter and he checked himself. "Now, as I was saying, this line shows where the edge was hardened. You need a hard steel cutting edge and you need a soft steel for the back. If it were soft all the way through it wouldn't hold an edge; if it were hard all the way through it'd snap as if it were made of glass. The old swordmakers used to cover the back of the blade with a coating of clay. The line is where the clay stopped. Then they'd heat the blade in a charcoal fire. The edge would become very hard and brittle, but the back would be protected and would stay soft and elastic, sort of a cushion. Notice how irregular the line is. In the newer blades the line's faked. It's very neat and regular and the blade's not worth a damn."

The colonel took the handle of the sword in both hands and swung the sword through the air. The sunlight glanced off the blade as off a jewel. A pair of passing marines stopped and watched, smiling slightly at the spectacle of the colonel, small and spiky looking, solemnly swinging the blade through great glittering arcs.

The colonel slipped the blade reluctantly into the lacquered scabbard. "Someday I'd like to have a chance to try this out. I'll bet it'd be like cutting butter." He turned away and marched briskly back into the tent. Witherspoon followed him, carrying the sword.

"Well, I guess that's that," the colonel said. "Why don't you go get yourself some chow? I want to see you after lunch."

Witherspoon fumbled in his pocket and brought out the little rectangles of gold embroidery he had snipped from the general's collar. "I thought you might like to have these, sir."

The colonel took General Matsui's collar tabs and laid them in the palm of his hand. The gold gleamed dully in the soft light of the tent. "Thanks. That was damn nice of you, Witherspoon."

Witherspoon went to his tent and lay on his cot until lunchtime. He went to the officers' mess tent and ate sparingly of corned beef, canned beans, and stewed prunes. He smoked a couple of cigarettes after lunch and then went back to the colonel's tent. Chernik and another clerk were pounding away on typewriters. The colonel was deep in the draft of a report. He looked up at Witherspoon and frowned.

"You said you wanted to see me after lunch, sir," Witherspoon reminded him.

"Now, look," the colonel said, "I'm not riding you or anything but I've got to send someone down to the stockade to weed out the POW's. You know what the setup is down there so you're our boy. That Nisei fellow, Murayama, can give you a hand. You can take off tomorrow morning. Go through the whole damned place and pull out all the soldiers. Maybe you can get Rossi to build you a separate cage for them. When you're satisfied that you've got them all, let me know and I'll send down a truck for them. Got that?"

Witherspoon nodded.

"Okay," the colonel said, "that's all."

Twelve

THE two men came down the road, away from the stockade. A haze of dust, golden in the late afternoon sunlight, hung over the stockade and drifted across the road to the marines' huts.

"Jesus Christ!" Swenson said. "Why'd he have to go and do that?"

"What did you expect him to do?" Mike asked, tired and irritable. He looked up at Swenson as if he expected an answer but there was none and they continued to walk toward their hut. Finally Mike spoke. "Kaneshiro looked as if he were going to cry."

Swenson grunted and asked, "Did Rossi leave anything? If we had the tubing we could rig up another still easy enough."

"It's all gone. There's nothing left but the kettles."

"Goddamn!" Swenson said. "I guess he really did a job on us."

They were approaching Rossi's hut and broke off their conversation until they were inside their own quarters. Swenson threw himself fully clad on his cot. He lay there, smoking, while Mike sat on his own cot and unlaced his boots.

"Anyway, Kaneshiro had enough liquor left to last us a couple of weeks," Swenson said. "Rossi didn't get that too, did he?"

Mike paused in the act of unbuttoning his dungaree jacket. "Rossi didn't get it but the stuff's gone. I've already talked with

Kaneshiro. He's pretty pissed off. He claims there won't be any more till we fix his still for him."

"He's lying," Swenson said. "I saw twenty full bottles yesterday. I'll break that old bastard's neck if he tries to hold out on me."

"You may get your own neck broken instead. The lieutenant's in a foul mood."

Swenson picked himself up from his cot and rummaged in the box at the foot of the cot for a pack of cigarettes. "It's not so much the liquor as the idea of the thing," he said. "If I make a deal with a gook, by God, he's going to keep his part of it." He opened the pack and lighted a cigarette and smoked thoughtfully. "I guess you and I are going to have to have a talk with Kaneshiro."

"I don't know," Mike said. "I don't like the looks of this thing. I don't want to take any more chances, not with the lieutenant all wound up the way he is."

"We're not taking any chances."

"I've been working my goddamn ass off today," Mike said, "and I'm telling you that Rossi isn't going to take any crap." He gave Swenson a detailed narrative of the events of the day. When he was through Swenson nodded gloomily. "I guess we've really been torpedoed."

Stripped down to his skivvies, Mike went to the door to let the evening breeze dry the sweat from his body. A minute later he came back into the room and fished under his cot for his helmet and a scrap of soap. "I found out one thing I didn't know before. Rossi visited the Madame last night."

Swenson whistled, a long, meaningful whistle, full of lewd understanding. "I wondered how long it was going to take him."

Mike grinned. "I guess he must have been pretty tanked up."

"I guess he must have been," Swenson agreed. As he mulled over this piece of information his previous moroseness gave way to an air of happy inspiration. "If he's been messing around with the Madame, I think we can take a chance ourselves. He won't be able to say much even if he does find out."

Mike, who had started for the door, stopped. "About what?"

"You got any idea where that liquor is?"

Mike answered reluctantly. "I have a lead but I don't know what it's worth. After I saw Kaneshiro I ran into the Madame. I guess she figured Kaneshiro had something to do with Rossi's cracking down on the cathouse. Anyway, she told me where she thinks Kaneshiro's hidden the liquor. I was in a hurry and I didn't have time to look."

Swenson stared out of the window. He saw the doctor come from his hut and set a kettle of water to heat over the earthenware stove. Loomis slouched by the window, whistling a melancholy air. From the stockade came the intermittent clanging of the cooks' metal spoons against the sides of the rice kettles.

"You think the Madame's giving us the straight poop?"

"I don't see why she wouldn't," Mike said.

Swenson looked thoughtful. "It looks to me like everything's all set up for us."

"Us?" Mike said. "I've told you I don't want any part of it."

"You're coming along with me," Swenson said. "After Rossi sacks out tonight we're going inside — gooks kicking up a racket or something. Taliaferro'll be at the gate and if anything happens he'll back us up." Swenson lay back on his cot, fully relaxed, and a faint smile played around his mouth. "I'd sure like to see that son of a bitch's face when he finds out that his liquor's gone."

It was almost dark when Kaneshiro's grandson hurried up the path, stopping for no one, his young face solemn with the weight of the message he carried. He scurried into a hut at the end of the path, panting from his long run and the excitement but when he faced his grandfather he halted and drew himself up at attention, or as close to attention as his excitement permitted. Kaneshiro went on with his work for a minute before turning to receive the boy's report.

"She told him," the boy said. "Gushiken sent me to tell you that she told him."

"I thought she would. What else did Gushiken say?"

"That's all," the boy said, crestfallen. "He said he had a very hard time with her. She was very stubborn, Gushiken said."

"Gushiken always does things the hard way," Kaneshiro said. He went back to his work and the boy settled down in a corner of the room and watched him.

Kaneshiro took an empty bottle and laid it near the doorway. He went outside and viewed it critically and moved it so that it couldn't be overlooked by anyone coming up the path. He came back into the house and laid a second bottle carelessly on its side halfway across the room. He took six more bottles and cached them in a corner of the room, artfully arranging a square of cloth over them so that their outlines were still visible.

"Anyone looking at them could tell what they were," the boy said. Kaneshiro nodded. He put the remaining bottles, a dozen in all, in a straw sack.

"Take these home. Hide them underneath the house. If anyone comes, let me know."

"Is it all right if I come back here later?" the boy asked hopefully.

"No. You stay and guard the house."

142

The boy lifted the sack of bottles to test its weight. The bottles clinked and he put the sack down hurriedly. "It's heavy," he said.

"You can carry it," Kaneshiro said.

Still the boy waited.

"Go on," Kaneshiro ordered.

"What are you going to do with him when you catch him?" the boy asked.

"Go on home," Kaneshiro said. "I don't know what you're talking about."

The boy hid the liquor under the house as he had been ordered to do, lingered long enough to lull any suspicion his grandfather might have, and then returned stealthily toward the hut at the end of the path.

He stationed himself in the bushes by the side of the path a hundred yards away from the hut. He ignored the first half-dozen people who passed him on the way home from the square to their dwellings. At last Gushiken lumbered up the path. He was carrying the handle from a hoe over his shoulder. A little later, Nadoyama and Mirata passed by, both carrying bamboo pikes, the points charred to hardness. Tomimura came, swinging a long club. The last to arrive was Arakaki, armed with one of the cooks' long iron spoons.

The boy crept closer to the hut to watch the men assembled in the courtyard. Kaneshiro had drawn up the remainder of the Special Attack Unit in its first formation since the disastrous retreat to the south. Only six were left, and they were none too sound. Nadoyama's arms and shoulders were burly with knotted muscle but his bleary eyes were closed almost tight from the trachoma that was slowly blinding him. Mirata had wasted away until his arms were hardly thicker than his bamboo staff. Tomimura, a gnome of a man, gray and wrinkled as a dried-up apple, leaned heavily on his club. The youngest of the squad, Arakaki, was a sturdy but stone-deaf recruit.

Kaneshiro allowed his men to fall out of ranks and they squatted gratefully on the ground and brought out their pipes. The Okinawans who lived in the other houses around the courtyard stayed inside, watching the proceedings from their doors and windows. The boy crept nearer and listened to the old men's conversation.

"Eh, General, how about a ration of whisky to settle my stomach?" squeaked the dwarf, Tomimura.

"Afterward," Kaneshiro said impatiently. "A ration all around, afterward."

The boy wriggled forward on his stomach. He scraped his chest on a pine root and held his breath until the sharp pain had subsided to a dull ache. Kaneshiro was pacing off the distance from the house to the other side of the path. The men were silent as they watched their leader make his preparations. The boy hugged the ground, his wide-open eyes taking in every movement. Nadoyama and Mirata began to talk in low voices of the days when they had carried their pikes in defense of their village, but Kaneshiro ordered them to be silent.

When it was almost dark, Kaneshiro sent his men to their posts. Tomimura was stationed behind the hut. Mirata guarded the left side of the yard and Nadoyama concealed himself behind the trees at the entrance to the courtyard. Arakaki, the deaf man, and Gushiken crossed to the other side of the path. Kaneshiro himself crouched behind a tree from where he could cover both the road and the house. He had armed himself with a long staff.

144

The boy worked his way even closer, feeling secure in the dark, but his foot caught in a dry tangle of brush. The noise brought Mirata on the run. He thrashed the underbrush with his pike and when the bamboo caught the boy a glancing blow he leaped on him and held him pinned to the groud. The boy emitted shrill yelps of pain that brought Kaneshiro, who dragged the boy to his feet and, holding him securely by his shirt, repeatedly struck him across his face with the flat of his horny old hand. The boy squirmed and blubbered for mercy until Kaneshiro released him. Kaneshiro followed the boy to the pathway, prodding him with the end of his staff, and watched until the slight figure had merged into the darkness of the night.

The old men took up their positions again, grumbling at the false alarm. The boy stopped fifty yards down the path and rubbed his tears into the dirt that covered his smarting cheeks. He thought of something he would need and darted into the square, where an extra length of rope for the well bucket hung in the galley shed. When he came back he made his preparations and settled down at the side of the road to await the next development. A woman bound on a nocturnal errand passed him, unaware of his presence. An inquisitive dog discovered him but he struck at it with the rope and the dog went howling down the road. There were no more disturbances and the boy grew drowsy from the long wait.

The intruders entered the stockade after the moon had risen high above the trees. Mike was carrying an empty carton. Swenson was armed with his club. They came up the path without making any attempt to muffle the noise of their progress. The boy crouched behind a tree, trembling with anticipation. His heart pounded until the night seemed to echo with the beats of a giant clock.

Kaneshiro uttered a signal like the croak of a frog. Swenson and Mike swung off the road, passing unchallenged between the hidden guards, and made for the house. The empty bottle on the doorsill was plainly visible in the moonlight. Swenson let out a restrained cry of exultation and turned his flashlight into the interior of the house. He and Mike entered the house and for a moment there was the clinking of the bottles and a low-voiced conversation. When they came out, Mike was carrying the carton, now filled with bottles, while Swenson carried a single bottle in his free hand. Kaneshiro permitted them to go as far as the gap between the trees before he sprang from behind his tree, brandishing his staff and screaming violent war cries.

Gushiken and the others fell on them from both sides and Mirata ran from behind the hut and attacked them from the rear. As the first blows fell on their shoulders, the two intruders broke and ran for the gate. Mike ran with his head down, his shoulders hunched over the heavy box he was carrying. Swenson covered the rear, swinging his club at his most dangerous assailant while he fended off attacks from other quarters with the bottle. Mirata and Tomimura were the first to fall under his blows. Nadoyama tripped over a root and put himself out of the skirmish. Arakaki was hit in the pit of the stomach by a wild swing of Gushiken's hoe handle and collapsed on the ground, gasping for breath. Swenson parried a blow of Kaneshiro's, fetched Gushiken a solid clout across his shoulders and turned and ran. Kaneshiro and Gushiken pursued them but their prey was faster and they lost ground steadily. Swenson saw them fall behind and caught up with Mike, who was streaking for the gate.

146

The boy saw the two men running toward him, one tall and the other crouched over. Behind them came his grandfather, forcing the last spurt of speed from his shrunken legs. The boy waited until the two fleeing men were almost abreast of him before he pulled the rope he held in his hand. The rope, taut between the boy's hand and a tree across the road, caught Mike and Swenson across the shins. They pitched forward onto the ground amid the sound of breaking glass. The boy, who had been jerked from his hiding place by the impact of their bodies on the rope, sprawled on the ground beside them. He scrambled to his feet just in time to avoid the first blows of Gushiken's hoe handle.

Thirteen

SWENSON had brought a clawhammer with him to loosen the nails that secured the wire to a corner post of the lunatics' cage. The nails were driven in solidly; Swenson had seen to that when his working party had raised a solid framework of heavy posts to replace the doctor's limp makeshift. But the slowness with which Swenson worked was due less to the strength of the nails than to the bruised muscles of his back. The doctor had patched up Swenson's cuts and abrasions but there was nothing he could do for the damage underneath the skin.

Smoky Joe and the two other men had crawled out from under the tarpaulin and now they shuffled through the dust toward the corner where Swenson was working. They said nothing but their eyes were on the hole Swenson was making in the side of the cage and they advanced steadily toward him until a sweep of the hammer sent them backward in alarm. Smoky Joe screamed with anger but the other two drifted away and turned their attention to Rossi and Kaneshiro, who stood outside the cage.

Wrapped securely around Rossi's hand was a rope that fastened Kaneshiro's wrists behind his back. Kaneshiro was watching Swenson but his face was impassive and his whole demeanor expressed utter indifference to the preparations that were being made. When Swenson had opened a gap in the wire large enough to admit Kaneshiro, Rossi jerked the rope and ordered the old man forward. Kaneshiro obeyed without hesitation. At the opening in the wire Kaneshiro stooped and prepared to enter but Rossi restrained him and, drawing his knife, cut the cord around his wrists. As soon as the old man was inside the cage Swenson began to nail up the wire.

The men in the cage backed away from Kaneshiro, who ignored them and crossed to the far corner of the cage. He stood there, facing the three lunatics, while Swenson finished sealing the only exit from the cage. Kaneshiro's composure was broken only by an occasional flicker of wariness in his eyes as he watched Smoky Joe, who came at him in a series of short rushes and retreats. The lunatic's attacks were accompanied by howls of indignation at the intrusion. He danced and gibbered and flung his arms about menacingly but he retreated before he came within striking distance. At last he ventured too close and Kaneshiro's fist lashed out and caught him on the chest. Smoky Joe howled and fled to the shelter of the tarpaulin. One of the two lunatics who were left approached Kaneshiro timidly, smiling with foolish friendliness, as if to make amends for Smoky Joe's behavior. He laid an exploratory hand on Kaneshiro's clean tunic, so much finer than his own greasy rags. Kaneshiro struck down his hand and the lunatic, hurt and bewildered, sighed piteously.

"Get a load of that, Lieutenant," Swenson said. "The nut's trying to make friends with him."

"When I told you to keep your mouth shut I meant it," Rossi said.

Smoky Joe had carried the news to the lunatics in the shelter of the tarpaulin. The geisha, attended by her girl accompanist, came into the open. Her face, which once had been firm and masklike, had sagged and the madness was showing in her wild eyes. Her kimono had been ripped and its gold brocade was heavily overlaid with dust. She knelt facing Kaneshiro and indicated that he should take a seat beside her. Kaneshiro remained standing. The geisha pleaded with him, begging him to join her, but the old man paid no attention to her. Her pleas became more urgent and her hands twisted in agitation. At last the old man could stand it no longer and uttered a single word.

"Damare!"

The geisha's discourse ceased as abruptly as if Kaneshiro had slapped her across the mouth. Her lips worked soundlessly for a moment and her face became contorted with anger. The silence was broken when she arose from the ground and gave vent to a stream of foul abuse. Kaneshiro stood firm. The two marines waited until the geisha had ended her tirade and retreated to the tarpaulin. Her companions followed her, leaving Kaneshiro alone in his corner of the cage.

Rossi and Swenson went down the path into the square, which was swarming with prisoners going to or coming from the galley. The prisoners parted to make a path for the two marines and stood aside and watched in silence as Rossi and Swenson passed among them.

"It doesn't look as if they're going to make any trouble today," Rossi said, stopping near the galley. "That ought to make it easier for you, Swenson."

Swenson nodded gloomily. "I wish I knew what the hell you were up to, Lieutenant. You have me by the balls and I know it. If you're going to break me, I wish you'd go ahead and get it done with. I've been broken before and I'm not going to bitch about it."

"I'm not interested in breaking you, not now at any rate. If you got everything that was coming to you, you'd spend the next ten years making little ones out of big ones. That can wait. Right now you're going to show these gooks that they can't jump one of my men and get away with it. You're going to keep moving and you're going to look busy and you're going to let these gooks know that you're too tough to mess around with."

Swenson waited.

"You know the old well?" Swenson did. It was half filled with dirt and rubble and had not been used since the Okinawans had come to the stockade. "Break out a working party of gooks and get it cleaned out. Mike'll be in there with you as soon as the doctor's through with him."

When Rossi turned to go to the gate Swenson struck off toward the huts. Disaster had overtaken him so swiftly that he had had no time to erect his customary defenses. Worst of all had been his apprehension as to how Rossi would deal with him. Now that his immediate punishment had been determined his confusion of mind gave way to anger. By the time he had reached the first courtyard he was in the grip of a cold and furious rage.

Three women were bent over a pot in which dirty clothing boiled in gray, scummy water. At the side of the courtyard, the garments they had already washed hung from a long bamboo pole suspended between two trees. A fourth woman sewed in a doorway. Two old men squatted in a corner, fashioning rice paddles from thin slats of wood. They all looked up when Swenson came into the courtyard and then went on with their work, hastily, as if they wanted to finish quickly and be off.

Swenson took a cigarette from his pocket and lighted it. The old men, incorrigible cadgers of any form of tobacco that could be shredded finely for their pipes, looked up, fleetingly greedy, but promptly lowered their eyes and went back to their work. Nobody came toward Swenson to whine for a cigarette from the pack he still held in his hand.

"What the hell's gotten into you gooks?" Swenson demanded. He was prepared to silence anyone who answered but none of the prisoners showed the least interest in him. Even the dogs ignored his presence.

"Goddammit! When I talk to you, jump!"

Nobody jumped. On the contrary, they continued with their tasks. Swenson bore down on the old men who went on hacking at the wood with their dull knives.

"Give me those knives," Swenson ordered. He went up to the old men and struck one of the knives to the ground. The other old man dropped his knife so that it lay with the first one. Swenson scooped up the knives and put them in his pocket.

"Shove off. Get out of here."

The old men held their ground unblinkingly. Swenson picked up the paddles they had already completed and broke them, splitting each one lengthwise in his strong hands. The old men made no protest.

Swenson turned to the laundry women.

"Break it up, you old bitches!"

The women looked up, narrow-eyed and hostile. Swenson kicked at the heavy iron pot in which the laundry bubbled. It rocked on its stone supports and then toppled. The clothes fell into the dust and a cloud of steam hissed from the suddenly quenched charcoal underneath. The women backed away and waited.

"Break it up," Swenson repeated, "break it up!"

Swenson turned his attention to the houses. He disturbed a child sleeping by the window and the child set up a fearful squalling. Swenson swore at the infant but it only wailed more loudly. He made a threatening gesture and the child crawled to the door and was rescued by one of the laundrywomen. The woman, holding the bawling child in her arms, remained in the doorway and watched Swenson ransack the house. Extra clothing and bedding which had been carefully folded was dragged from the closet and spilled on the floor. A small hoard of chipped rice bowls was knocked from its shelf and fell to the floor. The woman watched it all, saying nothing.

Swenson went on to the next house. His rage was beginning to burn itself out and he made only a perfunctory check of the other five houses in the courtyard to see if any able-bodied males were hiding inside. There were none.

But in the next courtyard he came on two candidates for his working party. Soon he had collected a full complement of laborers. Their faces were familiar; they had all served at one time or another in the labor gangs Kaneshiro had organized and they fell in mechanically behind Swenson and followed him to the gate.

Tucci, Fischer's companion in the unfortunate adventure with the two Okinawan women, was guarding the gate. Swenson watched Tucci's face closely, searching his features for an indication that Tucci was secretly gloating over his sergeant's disgrace. But Tucci, though young and often foolish, was wise enough to keep his face as solemnly stupid as if it were he and not Swenson who was guilty. Tucci passed the picks and shovels under the lowest strand of wire to the Okinawans. The Okinawans took the tools and shouldered them and waited for Swenson to lead the way.

"Mike come back from sick bay yet?" Swenson asked.

"No. The lieutenant wants to see him when he does." And still Tucci kept his composure. It was almost with a sense of disappointment that Swenson turned away and led the laborers toward the well.

When Swenson regained the shelter of the trees he was sweating freely. The sweat stung the raw welts on his shoulders and soaked the dressings that covered the open cuts on his back. The working party proceeded briskly toward the well, the laborers silent and resigned to a day of heavy work. A boy ran onto the path suddenly and almost collided with Swenson. It was Kaneshiro's grandson. He faced Swenson for a moment, paralyzed with terror, but the puppy that was bound at his heels, the same spotted puppy that Swenson had once rescued from its tormentors, continued to yap cheerfully. Swenson grabbed the boy by his shoulder when he turned to run.

"Where do you think you're going, bub?"

The boy strained to get away, tugging at Swenson's hand on his shoulder. "Take it easy," Swenson said. "I'm not going to hurt you." The boy was recovering his breath and his terror seemed to abate with the change in Swenson's manner. Swenson eased his grip and extended a hand toward the puppy.

"How you coming along, you old pup?"

The puppy barked joyously and snapped at his fingers.

Swenson was delighted. "Hey, hey, that's the way, boy." He held the puppy lightly around its muzzle and the dog braced its four feet on the ground and backed away, growling mightily.

Swenson suddenly let go and the puppy tumbled head over heels and then came racing back for more.

"Say, you got a good dog there," Swenson told the boy. "You take the right sort of care of him and he'll make you a real good dog."

The boy twisted away and ran through the trees. The puppy, who had been playing around Swenson's feet, dashed after him. Swenson watched until they had disappeared.

"Ah, the goddamn gook kid," he said. "The goddamn gook."

Fourteen

THE Madame reached inside her blouse and brought out a paper packet and offered it to Kaneshiro.

"I've brought you a present," she said.

Kaneshiro, surly and uncommunicative, remained sitting on his heels in a corner of the cage, watching his visitor with unconcealed suspicion. The Madame tossed the packet to him. Kaneshiro let it lie on the ground, but Smoky Joe came after it and Kaneshiro hastened to snatch it out of his reach. Smoky Joe backed away and circled around Kaneshiro, as attentive as a dog after a bone. Kaneshiro opened the packet gravely and a brief flicker of pleasure crossed his face when he saw what it contained. He poured a little of the fine tobacco into his hand and rubbed it in his palm before pouring it back and putting the package on the ground between his feet.

"I am very grateful to you for your many favors but, unfortunately, I appear to have stupidly neglected to bring my pipe with me," he said with ironic pomposity but real bitterness.

"Eh, eh, how stupid of me," the woman cried.

She reached inside her blouse again and extracted a pipe which she passed through the wire to Kaneshiro. A box of matches followed the pipe. Kaneshiro accepted the presents gratefully and immediately filled the tiny bowl of the pipe. Smoky Joe came closer while Kaneshiro was busy lighting his pipe and again tried to steal the tobacco. Kaneshiro swung his fist and barely missed him and the lunatic backed away to a safe distance. Kaneshiro succeeded in lighting the pipe and smoked with relish.

"Thank you very much."

"It was nothing."

The Madame waited patiently for Kaneshiro to finish smoking.

"How are you getting along?"

"Not too badly," Kaneshiro answered, but he pointed to Smoky Joe and his voice suddenly broke into an old man's complaining whine. "This crazy man is after me all the time."

He knocked the morsel of dottle from the pipe and filled the bowl again with tobacco, smoking in silence until he had regained his composure.

"Why did you bring these presents?"

"It was the least I could do." The Madame spoke disarmingly but Kaneshiro looked at her narrowly; their old hostility lay clear and well defined just below their words, a smooth rock barely covered by shallow water.

"How are things down below?"

The Madame shrugged. "The sergeant was in the stockade this morning looking much the same as ever."

"I made a mistake," Kaneshiro said. "It was stupid."

"Yes, it was stupid."

It was Kaneshiro's turn to shrug. "I'm a patient man but there comes a time when I simply can't put up with any more. I was a soldier. If I had died, that would have been an end to it."

157

The Madame, unimpressed by Kaneshiro's stoicism, turned her attention to Smoky Joe, who was glowering at them from under the matted hair that hung almost over his eyes.

"Who was he?"

"I don't know. A field worker probably. Look at his hands." Smoky Joe's hands, which were hanging loosely at his side, were square and stubby and covered with thick, horny callouses.

"How long has he been here?"

"From the beginning. I helped catch him and tie him up."

"Look at him," the Madame said, "his face, his eyes, the way he stands. More like an animal than a man."

Kaneshiro said nothing.

"I wonder how long they'll leave you here."

"Not long enough for that. I was a soldier and I know how to die."

"It will be interesting to watch."

"I'm sure you will enjoy it," Kaneshiro said gravely.

"Yes, that's true. I will."

"Go away," Kaneshiro ordered, with a resurgence of his customary domineering manner. "Go away, you stupid woman."

"Not yet," the Madame said. "I still have some business here."

Smoky Joe had sidled within arm's length and Kaneshiro sprang to his feet and in a sudden burst of energy drove him off. The lunatic fled but when Kaneshiro resumed his seat in the corner of the cage, he took up his position as before.

"Go away," Kaneshiro said. "Go away and leave me alone. A man can die in peace."

"Be patient," the Madame said. "I'm going, but first there's another old friend I came to visit."

The Madame went to the tarpaulin and called inside. "Oh,

Midori-san, are you at home? This is Shirayuki, come to visit you."

There was no answer from within the tent and the Madame called again. In a moment the geisha crawled into the sunlight. Her clothing was disheveled and the top of her kimono hung loosely from her shoulders, exposing flat, withered breasts. Lank, uncombed hair hung over her haggard face. She stared without recognition at the Madame, who began to chatter in a lively manner.

"It's Shirayuki from down the street, Midori-san. Don't you remember how you used to pass my house when you were on your way to entertain the general? I remember how busy we used to be with the lieutenants and captains when we'd see you hurrying down the street on the way to a party at headquarters. We all used to envy you; why, I used to tell my girls that if they minded their manners and learned to dance and sing instead of carrying on with those drunken lieutenants they might be waiting on a general themselves some day."

The Madame sighed and smiled in a friendly way at her listener. "Oh, yes, I remember that well. Of course, there were times when I entertained the general myself. But you didn't know about that; I know you didn't think much of me and I can't say that I blame you."

She broke off and inspected the geisha's face. The geisha stared at her visitor with eyes that showed the dim reflections of tortured memories running through the twisted brain.

"Why, Midori-san, you're not looking well at all. Were you up too late last night? Come, come, you ought to pull yourself together. It's broad daylight you know and you shouldn't be going around half-naked. If the general could see you now, he'd hardly recognize you."

The geisha stared back dully.

"Come, come," the Madame urged, "you really ought to take better care of yourself."

The geisha shook herself and lifted a hand to pull the hair back over her neck. She drew her kimono closer about her, covering her breasts and her knees. The Madame bobbed her head in approval.

"Why, that's much better. You're looking more like your old self now. Come, I want you to meet an old friend of mine. He's come to stay with you for a while and I hope you'll treat him as an honored guest."

The geisha went to the corner of the cage where Kaneshiro crouched. Smoky Joe, who had continued to keep watch while the Madame talked, moved aside for the geisha, who halted a few feet from Kaneshiro. Her face, which had maintained an expression of puzzled incomprehension, suddenly became animated.

"A spy!" she shrieked in a terrible harsh voice. "I know you, Haraguchi, you've come to spy on me again." Her long, ragged fingernails reached for Kaneshiro's throat. Kaneshiro struck her arms away in a panic.

"Get away from me, you crazy old woman. I'm not Haraguchi."

The geisha retreated out of reach of Kaneshiro's arms, but Smoky Joe came from behind her and approached Kaneshiro.

"Go away!" Kaneshiro roared, striking a warning blow that caught the lunatic on the shoulder. While Smoky Joe was off balance, Kaneshiro lunged forward between him and the Madame and crossed the enclosure, halting with his back against the wire at the other side of the cage.

"Stay away!" he yelled, "stay away from me, you lunatics!"

160

The noise brought the other inmates from under the tent into the bright sunlight. They crawled out into the enclosure, five unkempt men and the girl who accompanied the geisha. With mounting terror Kaneshiro watched them converge on his corner of the cage.

"Good-by," the Madame called mockingly. "Good-by, Kaneshiro-san. I'm late and I have to hurry."

Fifteen

NOBODY was in sight except the guard at the gate when Corcoran swung the jeep to a stop in front of the main gate and permitted Witherspoon to alight. The guard was a dark-faced man whom Witherspoon hadn't seen before. He looked at Witherspoon suspiciously, not rising from the box where he sat. Witherspoon explained that he was looking for Lieutenant Rossi.

The guard motioned inside the stockade. "He's busy."

"I guess I'd better go in and find him." Witherspoon stepped toward the gate but the guard warned him away with his rifle. "You can't go in there. I got my orders."

"How am I going to find the lieutenant?" Witherspoon asked reasonably.

"I don't know. I got my orders," the guard repeated.

"Who'll you take orders from to let me in?"

"The lieutenant."

"But he's already inside."

"Sergeant of the guard."

"Where's the sergeant of the guard?"

The guard looked beyond Witherspoon toward the marines' quarters. "He's coming."

Witherspoon turned and saw Taliaferro approaching them.

162

Taliaferro didn't look pleased when he saw who the visitor was, but he was civil enough.

"I don't know how long the lieutenant's going to be in there," he said. "You want me to go in and find him?"

"I'd just as soon go in myself," Witherspoon said. "I've never had a good look at the stockade."

Taliaferro told Witherspoon how to find his way to the old well where he would probably find Lieutenant Rossi. The guard still barred the way. Witherspoon looked inquiringly at Taliaferro.

"What's the matter, Fischer?" Taliaferro asked.

"Nobody's given me any orders to let this officer in," Fischer said.

"Let him in," Taliaferro said. "He's all right."

"Is that an order?"

"It's an order," Taliaferro said.

Fischer removed the bar from the gate and grudgingly opened it for Witherspoon. "I ain't taking any chances," Fischer muttered, "not the way you and Swenson been riding me."

Witherspoon had gone a few yards into the square when he heard Taliaferro call to him. "Say, Lieutenant, we going to go gook-hunting again?"

"Not this time," Witherspoon said. "My business is with the prisoners in the stockade."

"I was beginning to get worried," Taliaferro said. "Last time you gave me a hell of a scare." Taliaferro grinned and Witherspoon turned away and went on into the square.

Witherspoon was surprised that his arrival didn't create more of a stir among the Okinawans. He had heard stories told by other Japanese-speaking officers of their experiences with friendly civilians and it puzzled and alarmed him that these

163

prisoners rebuffed his overtures so firmly. He hurried away from them toward the path that Taliaferro had told him to take to the well. He had gone a couple of hundred yards when he saw Rossi coming toward him.

"My God!" Rossi exclaimed. "The one-man raider battalion again!"

Witherspoon knew now that whenever he came among the marines at the stockade his presence would evoke memories of his defection in the cave. The humiliating knowledge appalled him. He tried to smile, but it was a sickly effort.

"What are you after this time?"

"The colonel's given me another job."

"Wasn't he satisfied with the job you did last time? What's he trying to do, get us all killed?"

There was little Witherspoon could do except to try to change the direction of the conversation. "Can you put me and my driver up for a while? We'll probably be here a few days."

"If the doctor doesn't mind having you, you can move in with him. Your driver knows where he can find a sack."

Witherspoon explained why he had returned to the stockade. "It's about time," Rossi said, "but how do you expect to go about it? These gooks look all the same to me."

"The first thing to do is to get together all the men of the right age. Then I'll have to interrogate them one by one. It looks like a pretty tedious job. I was wondering if I could borrow your interpreter; he's probably had some experience at this sort of thing."

Rossi considered the request for a moment. "You can have him if you promise to work the hell out of him. You'll find him with Swenson at the well. As long as you keep him on his feet

164

and keep him working you can do anything you like with him."

"What's the matter?" Witherspoon asked. "Has Mike gotten himself in trouble?"

"He's in trouble all right," Rossi said, but since he didn't seem disposed to elaborate on the subject Witherspoon let the conversation drop and went on toward the well alone.

He found Swenson supervising the erection of a primitive hoist over the well. Mike was not in sight. Swenson had evidently put on a burst of energy when he had heard someone coming but when he saw who it was he slackened his pace, looking disgruntled, as if he were disappointed that Witherspoon was not Rossi.

"You've come back, Lieutenant," Swenson said.

Witherspoon admitted that he had. Mike's head appeared over the side of the well. He looked tired and the skin of his face was gray. "Are you coming back to make some more trouble, Lieutenant?" He moved one leg painfully as he came out of the well. "I've got enough trouble today."

"Ever since we've been here the gooks have been getting along without this well," Swenson said. "Now the lieutenant says we got to clean it out. Ain't that a load of chickenshit?" He turned his back on Witherspoon and threatened the Okinawans, who had stopped working.

"I hate to tell you this," Witherspoon said, "but Lieutenant Rossi said I could borrow Mike. I guess you'll have to carry on alone, Sergeant."

"Private'll do," Swenson said without turning around. "He hasn't broken me yet but I'm not counting on anything."

Mike's boots were covered with a thick clayey mud from the bottom of the well. He sat on the ground and scraped it off with a stick while Witherspoon waited. "This job of yours,

Lieutenant, does it mean I'm going to have to walk around or is it something I can do sitting down?"

"I'm afraid we're going to have to do some walking," Witherspoon said. "Why?"

"My back's killing me," Mike said, getting to his feet with painful care.

Witherspoon explained his mission while he and Mike walked back down the path. "Its going to be a hell of a lot of work," Mike said. "We're going to have to go through the whole stockade ourselves looking for the kind of men you want to talk to."

"I was wondering, couldn't one of the Okinawans round up the men of the right age for us? Isn't there a headman?"

"There was," Mike said, "but there isn't any more. He ended up in the booby hatch."

"That's too bad," Witherspoon said seriously. "What happened to him?"

"It's a long story," Mike said, "and I'd just as soon not go into it now. We might as well start out here." He turned into one of the courtyards but they found only a couple of old men in addition to the women and the ever-present children.

They found their first candidate two courtyards away. He was a stocky young fellow with three fingers missing from his right hand, but the stumps were freshly healed and the wound might have been incurred in the line of duty. They went from courtyard to courtyard, sometimes finding only young boys and old men and sometimes picking up two or three likely men at a time. After an hour the total number came to almost two dozen.

The prisoners followed Witherspoon in a ragged file, with Mike at the rear to urge on the stragglers. Witherspoon led them to the galley and allowed them to squat in the shade among the cook pots, but Mike suggested that it would be better if they waited in the sun outside the galley shed. They were remarkably quiet and followed Mike's orders obediently, rising from their squatting positions on the ground and moving and then squatting again. They talked hardly at all among themselves and seemed to have no desire to learn why they had been chosen from all the other Okinawans in the stockade.

Mike made a crude desk of some boards supported on two rice kettles. When Witherspoon was ready with his paper and pencil Mike raised his hand and called for the first prisoner to come to the table. It was the man with the missing fingers. He was ill at ease and fidgeted wretchedly while Mike looked him up and down.

"Name?"

"Kamiya Toshio."

"Rank?"

Kamiya looked embarrassed. He smiled uncertainly. "I don't have any rank. I'm just a farmer."

Mike waved the explanation aside. "Where do you come from?"

"Okinawa. My father owned a farm on the Motobu peninsula. We needed money and so I signed up to come and work here."

"All right, all right. Did you ever work for the Japanese army?"

"No."

"Why not?" Mike's voice had suddenly become harsh. "The Japanese used every able-bodied person they could get hold of. What was the matter with you?"

167

The man sighed. "I worked for the army. So did everyone else. We couldn't help it."

"All right," Mike said. "We don't care if you worked for the army or not, but make sure that you tell us the truth. What happened to your hand?"

Kamiya began to show more assurance. "It was after the army retreated to the escarpment. I was with some people from my village. We were trying to get south and find a cave to hide in. It was hot and my aunt was having trouble with the bundle she was carrying. She couldn't carry it any farther but she wouldn't leave it, and while I was arguing with her the guns began firing. The old woman was killed and I lost part of my hand."

Mike nodded and turned to Witherspoon. "Do you have any questions?"

"No, he looks all right to me," Witherspoon said. Mike dismissed Kamiya and told him to wait on the other side of the galley, away from the rest of the prisoners. Mike called the next man, and then the next, and there was little variety in their stories. Mike did all the talking. Witherspoon sat beside him, writing down the prisoners' names and listening to the questions and answers, but the flow of Japanese was so swift that he soon gave up trying to do more than follow the bare outline of the dialogue. It was not at all like Miss Ito's conversation class at language school. The shed was hot and Mike repeated the questions monotonously. Witherspoon became drowsy and shook himself to clear his head.

A crop-haired boy, so young that Witherspoon would have left him behind if it had not been for Mike's insistence, was called and came on the double. When he was in front of the table he snapped to attention and remained in that strained posture until the questioning was over.

"Name?"

"Yamazaki Yoshisaburo."

"Rank?"

"Second-class Private." Witherspoon was jolted into awareness. His body went tense, as if he expected something violent to happen, but Mike's unimpassioned voice droned on without a break in the routine of questioning.

"Unit?"

"Ishida Battery, Third Independent Mountain Artillery Battalion."

"Your duties?"

"Gunner."

"When were you captured?"

"I wasn't captured. I threw away my uniform and joined the civilians."

"You've been captured right now," Mike told him. "Don't you know you could have been shot as a spy? Why didn't you turn yourself in?"

"Nobody asked me," Yamazaki said.

"That's all for now," Mike told him. The boy followed Mike's instructions and sat down behind them.

The three remaining prisoners were quickly disposed of. They all claimed to be farmers and admitted under questioning only that they had been forced to work as laborers for the Japanese. All the prisoners but the boy were now in a group on the other side of the galley. The boy Yamazaki sat in the dust, his sharp-featured face calm and resigned, and yet marked with pride and contempt for the farmers and laborers who waited in the sun.

Witherspoon and Mike stood up, Mike favoring his right leg and holding his back stiff and straight.

"I guess that about does it," Witherspoon said. "And the only one we got was the one I would have sworn couldn't have been a soldier. I suppose we might as well take them back."

"Wait," Mike said. He limped over to where the prisoners were and ordered them to stand. They got to their feet easily and stood relaxed, waiting for the order that would release them.

Mike turned his back on them and spoke to Witherspoon, who had joined him. "I'm going to try an old gag. Watch them." He remained facing Witherspoon for a moment and then he swung about suddenly so that he faced the prisoners and snapped to attention.

"*Kiwotsuke!*"

One of the four prisoners who were trapped by the order was Kamiya, the man with the missing fingers who had admitted to being a laborer. His heels came together and his feet pointed out at a rigid angle; the muscles in his calves and thighs tightened until he felt pain; his stomach was sucked in; his shoulders wrenched back; and his chin ground into his chest. He stood at attention until the realization of what he had done came over him and he dropped his head and stared at the ground.

Kamiya and the three others were called back to the make-shift table. Mike undertook their interrogation again, his voice flat and impersonal, and Witherspoon wrote down what he could gather from the rapid Japanese of the prisoners. When they were through the prisoners joined the boy, who glanced at them indifferently.

"That was a good idea," Witherspoon said. "I don't know that I would have thought of it."

170

"It was simple," Mike said. "It usually works if you catch them off guard. They can't help themselves."

They let the civilians go but they took the soldiers to the gate and made them squat inside the wire. The soldiers settled down without any grumbling, readjusting themselves easily to the familiar routine of meaningless orders. Besides Kamiya and Yamazaki there was a corporal, a sturdy, bandy-legged man with an intelligent, strong-featured face, and two privates. Fischer, who was still on guard, demanded ill-naturedly that the prisoners be moved farther away from the gate. The corporal asserted his authority by relaying Mike's order to move in a sharp, parade-ground voice.

Rossi came to the gate to look over the prisoners. "When I see these sad sacks," he said, "I wonder how they've managed to kill so many good men. They sure as hell don't look like soldiers." And it was true that, except for the corporal, they were a most unprepossessing group. "How many do you think you're going to get in all?"

"I don't know. Twenty or thirty, maybe."

"We'll have to string some wire around them," Rossi said. He went into the stockade and drew a line on the ground, making a square around the prisoners. "Until we get the wire up that'll have to do." He turned to Fischer. "One step over that and you shoot."

Fischer's face showed that the order would be carried out scrupulously.

Coming out of the stockade Rossi brushed against Mike, who was leaning against a gatepost.

"What's the matter with you?" Rossi asked. "You look like hell."

"I feel lousy, Lieutenant. Can I go to sick bay?"

"Of course you feel lousy," Rossi said. "You let a couple of gooks beat the be-jesus out of you last night. I wouldn't be surprised if you feel a lot worse before the day's over. No, you can't go to sick bay. The doctor's already looked at you and he says you'll recover."

"It's my stomach," Mike said. "I think I'm going to be sick."

"It won't kill you," Rossi said. "If you start puking you can go see the doctor. Until then you keep on your feet and keep working. Lieutenant Witherspoon'll see that you don't goof off."

"I didn't come up here as a guard," Witherspoon protested. "We've already gotten a good start on this job. The rest can wait until Mike feels up to it."

Rossi said, "He's going to stay in there, sick or not, for a damn good reason. If you don't want him, I'll send him back with Swenson."

"All right," Witherspoon said. "I'll see that he stays on the job."

Ten minutes later, as they were walking along a path among the huts, Mike was violently sick. When he had sufficiently recovered, Witherspoon helped him up the hill toward sick bay.

Mike was the first person to arrive at sick bay, even though it was long after the hour when the prisoners usually lined up for treatment. The doctor was sitting in the sunlight, looking down the path with a worried expression on his face, while Loomis busied himself cleaning up inside. A patient in the ward complained fitfully but the nurse wasn't there to attend to her and Loomis didn't bother.

172

The doctor nodded to Witherspoon, but he immediately turned his attention to Mike, leading him inside to the operating table, a crude affair nailed together from salvaged lumber. Witherspoon felt a quick release of tension; he realized that he had been expecting to be reminded again of his behavior in the cave.

"What the hell have you been up to, Mike?" the doctor asked. "I told you to take it easy today."

Mike rolled over on his side and hung his head over the edge of the table. He retched and doubled up as the muscles in his belly tightened convulsively. When his muscles had relaxed Mike lay back on the table, breathing more easily. He wiped the sweat from his forehead and let his legs fall back loosely on the table.

"How long has this been going on?" the doctor asked.

"About twenty minutes ago I began to feel sick. I was in the stockade with the lieutenant."

"What were you doing in the stockade? I told you to take it easy. You don't have any business running around the stockade in your condition."

"Lieutenant Rossi sent Swenson and me into the stockade with a working party to clear out the old well. I didn't think I was in a position to argue with him."

"I don't care what the circumstances are," the doctor said, "nobody has any business making a sick man do heavy work." He turned to his small shelf of drugs and selected a bottle. "When a man gets sick I begin giving the orders."

Nobody contradicted him.

The doctor filled a small glass with a milky liquid. "Here's something for your stomach. I'm going to keep you up here for the rest of the day. Don't worry, Rossi can't do anything about it. There's nothing the matter with you that a little rest won't fix up and I'm going to see that you get it. Bring me a blanket, Loomis."

Loomis brought the blanket and while Mike sat upright on the edge of the table the doctor and Loomis spread the blanket over the hard boards, folding it at the head so that it formed a sort of pillow. Mike lay back gratefully.

"I just feel sort of shot," he said.

"That's all right," the doctor said. "We'll take care of you."

He went outside again and he and Witherspoon sat down. Loomis went back to his work, still silent. Mike closed his eyes and in a few minutes he was asleep.

"Have you been around the stockade today?" the doctor asked. Witherspoon explained what he had been doing.

"What's going on down there anyway?" the doctor asked. "Something's brewing — I haven't had a single patient come up here yet. These people don't like going to see a doctor anyway, but there's usually enough of them in pain so that they come up here whether they like it or not."

"I don't know what's going on," Witherspoon said, "and I wish you'd explain a few things to me. Everybody seems to have something on his mind that I don't know about. Rossi told me that Mike had gotten in some sort of trouble but I still don't know what it's all about."

The doctor told him about the disputed liquor and Kaneshiro's trap and how Swenson and Mike had rushed to the gate, covered with blood and dirt and stinking of bad liquor. And he also told Witherspoon how Rossi had caught Kaneshiro and put him in the cage with the lunatics to punish him for the success of his revenge.

"My God!" Witherspoon said. "This is a real mess, isn't it?"

"It's a mess all right. I don't know how Rossi feels about this, but the danger signal as far as I'm concerned is when patients refuse to come to sick bay. A man will do a lot of things to gain a point of principle, or just out of stubbornness, but it takes more than a point of principle for a woman to deliberately keep her sick baby away from a doctor. I thought I was getting to know these people and I thought they liked me. I don't know what to make of this."

They were silent for a while, smoking and watching a goat that had come from the brush at the side of the path. The goat looked at them with a look of infinite surprise and then turned and leaped back into the shrubbery.

Loomis came out and sat beside them. "Mike's gone to sleep," he said.

Witherspoon looked back into the room. Mike had rolled over onto his stomach and was sleeping comfortably, his arms hanging over the sides of the table.

"How do you figure this, Loomis?" the doctor asked.

"I don't," Loomis said. "If some damn fool gets himself beaten up by a crazy gook I'll do my best to patch him up, but don't ask me to tell you how or why he got himself messed up or what's going to come of it. I'll take care of anyone who comes up here, white man or gook, I don't give a damn, but if they don't want to come I don't give a damn either."

"That isn't quite what I had in mind," the doctor said. "There's fifty to sixty people in this stockade who ought to be coming to sick bay. What's keeping them away? Do you think they're simply so outraged about what's happened to Kaneshiro that they're deliberately denying themselves medical care? I doubt it."

Witherspoon hunched over and took a stone and drew a

175

meaningless design in the dust. "I've been told that these people have been filled with stories about the terrible things the Americans would do to them — about how the marines on Guadalcanal ran over wounded prisoners with bulldozers and things like that. They've probably decided that what they knew was going to happen all the time is finally happening. Maybe they're staying home because they think they're all going to be killed anyway."

The doctor was not satisfied with Witherspoon's theory. "Why should these people worry about brutality? They've been exposed to it all their lives. For that matter, our own record isn't lily white. I don't say it all cancels out; what I'm getting at is that once they're jolted out of their civilized ways people don't really care about brutality. I've practiced in all sorts of places and learned to take things as they come. I don't like getting tangled up in moral issues; my business, like Loomis's, is to try to keep my patients from dying before their time. If I started worrying about right and wrong I'd be inclined to let a lot of my patients die on the grounds that the rest of us would be better off without them. The world comes in all shades of gray and I'm willing to accept it as it is. But, I know brutality when I see it and I don't like it. Still, I don't know if simple brutality has much to do with this."

Witherspoon tossed the stone he had been writing with into the bushes. "Anyway, it doesn't seem to have become very serious yet."

"No, not yet. What I'm worried about is what it may grow into. At any rate, it's only Rossi who can put an end to it. Rossi's in the driver's seat — if he knows what he's doing this whole thing will probably blow over. If he doesn't, God only knows what can happen."

The doctor rose and went inside and Witherspoon followed him. Mike stirred and shifted his position painfully.

"My goddamn back hurts like hell," he muttered, opening one eye and grimacing.

"It's going to bother you for a couple more days," the doctor said. "It'll hurt but nothing's broken and as long as it doesn't get infected you'll be as good as new. I'll have another look at you tonight."

Witherspoon was reminded of part of his conversation with Colonel Smith. "I almost forgot to tell you," he said to the doctor. "Colonel Smith up at Division thinks your military government team is going to come ashore and take over in a couple of days. It makes a difference, doesn't it? The whole business will be out of your hands before long."

But the doctor didn't respond as Witherspoon had expected. He was silent for a moment, frowning, and then he began to laugh gently. "I'm glad I'm going to be around," he said. "They'll probably put the Public Safety Officer to work to straighten out this mess. He used to be a police chief in a town in South Carolina."

Sixteen

FISCHER was on guard at post number four, on the hill behind the stockade. If there had been more light he could have
looked down onto the house where Swenson had once been
entertained by the Madame; as it was, the darkness behind the
wire was impenetrable except when the clouds that were flying
across the moon broke for an instant. Fischer sat on a box, his
rifle lying across his knees with the muzzle pointing into the
stockade at the height of a man's groin.

Fischer had reason to be thoroughly tired of standing guard.
Since the day when Swenson had caught him and Tucci with
the women it seemed that he was barely allowed to fall asleep
before a voice called him out to stand guard again. Fischer was
not given to introspection and yet, in spite of the tedium of
constant guard duty, he recognized the sense of well-being that
had come over him since Swenson's fall from grace. It was
Swenson's perfidy that had rankled — the repeated promises
of a woman of his own and then the sudden betrayal to Rossi
when all he had done was less by a thousand times than the sum
of Swenson's own irregularities.

He was aware in his dim way that the mood of the stockade
had changed. He listened in vain for the usual night sounds:
the fretful cries of the children, the muted voices of old men
arguing in a nearby hut, the quick burst of a woman's laughter

178

on which he would construct improbable fantasies that made the night pass faster and at the same time made his detention at the guard post more intolerable. Fischer's nerves were not notably delicate but he shifted his rifle uneasily and peered into the darkness as if searching for some reassurance that there was life inside the wire. But a great dark cloud, silvery at its very edges, was passing over the moon and there were only the thin lines of the wire in front of him and the dark mass of the trees against the sky.

Fischer knew that there had been trouble. He had heard the sounds of fighting inside the stockade and afterward he had been told how Swenson and Mike had been set upon by the Okinawans who had supplied them with liquor. He had seen Loomis swabbing out the cuts on Swenson's back with alcohol while Mike, spitting blood from his mouth, awaited his turn. And in the morning he had seen Kaneshiro, his hands bound behind him, marching across the square between Swenson and Rossi on the way to the lunatics' cage. The business at the gate with the prisoners-of-war had confirmed Fischer's belief that somewhere a cog had slipped. The knowledge gave him a perverse satisfaction.

A noise to his left drew Fischer's attention. He swung his rifle toward the sound, which even in the dark he knew came from among a clump of pines where dead needles lay thick and brown on the ground. The rustling was not repeated, but a little later a sound like a twig cracking came from another quarter. Fischer strained his senses, waiting for a burst of moonlight. The rustling began again, this time to the right of where it had started. Fischer judged the source of the noise to be some twenty yards directly in front of him. He let the safety off his rifle and waited.

When the moonlight broke suddenly over the trees, Fischer saw a stunted figure in the shadow of the trees. It looked to him like one of the Okinawans, crouching on the ground, waiting to spring at him. He fired once and then again and then once more before the clouds closed over the moon.

Taliaferro plodded wearily up the hill toward where Fischer sat, still covering the spot where he had seen his target.

"Goddammit," Taliaferro swore softly, "you characters are as trigger-happy as a bunch of deer hunters tonight. What's the trouble?"

Fischer tapped him on the shoulder and pointed into the stockade. "Something in there," he whispered. "I think I got it." He held his rifle ready while Taliaferro peered inside.

"There's something lying there all right," Taliaferro said. "I can just about make it out."

They waited, Fischer with his rifle and Taliaferro with a pistol, watching the barely discernible dark heap that lay on the ground inside the wire. It didn't move, nor did it make any sound.

Taliaferro pointed his flashlight toward the object and pressed the switch.

"A goat!" he cried, his voice rising in relief and anger. "Goddamn you, Fischer, when're you going to get yourself squared away?"

Fischer still held his rifle on the goat, as if the dead animal might rise up and be transformed into a live enemy. "It looked like a gook," he insisted. "It looked like a scrunched-up little gook who was figuring to jump me."

Taliaferro turned off his flashlight and put it in his pocket. "Ah, you meathead, Fischer."

"It looked like a scrunched-up little gook," Fischer began, but Taliaferro cut him off. "At least you're not seeing them a whole platoon at a time. Davis claims there was a whole mess of Japs moving around behind him. He says he could have gotten a couple of them but he figured the rest would have cut his throat before he could have got any more."

"There ain't no Japs around here," Fischer said.

"I know that, meathead," Taliaferro said impatiently. "Davis knows it too. Why the hell is he getting his ass in an uproar about it?"

"If they'd been Japs, they would've — "

"Davis knows they weren't Japs. What the hell are you guys so damned edgy about tonight? Maybe you want me to send Lieutenant Rossi up here to hold your hand?"

"I tell you it looked like — "

"I know," Taliaferro said. "It looked like a scrunched-up little gook who was figuring to jump you. I've got that straight. I don't want to hear about it any more. I'm going down and get myself a cup of java."

He started down the path. Fischer had just lost his outline in the general darkness when the sound of voices came from farther up the mountain. The voices, violent but thin because of the distance, rose in anger. They ended abruptly, with a long, wailing shriek that might have come from either a man or a woman.

Then there was silence until Fischer heard Taliaferro's voice from down the trail.

"Something going on up at the cage."

"Yeah," Fischer said, feeling that the alarm he had raised had in some way been justified by the disturbance, "I guess the nuts are acting up tonight."

181

Taliaferro grunted and went on down the trail. The sound of his feet in the rubble that lay along the trail had hardly died away when Fischer heard the geisha begin to sing.

Rossi and the doctor also heard the shriek and the geisha's song. Even Witherspoon, who was already asleep on a borrowed cot in the doctor's room, must have heard the geisha for he raised an arm and moved it across his face. The song went on, its melody so distorted by the singer's madness that it was close to a prolonged animal howl. The doctor waited until the geisha's voice had died away before he spoke.

"It lasted longer than usual. Besides, there was that shrieking before she began. It sounds like there's something wrong in the cage."

"They've acted up like that before." Rossi cut the deck of cards and began dealing a hand of seven-card stud. "Jack bets a nickel." He tossed a cardboard counter between the two hands. The doctor mechanically matched the bet.

"Has anybody been up to the cage since this morning?"

"Only the gook who takes them their food." Two more cards were dealt face up. "Ace bets," Rossi said, indicating a card in the doctor's hand. The doctor tossed another counter into the pot.

"I don't suppose the guard can see what's going on."

"No," Rossi said. "He's too far away and, anyway, it's dark. It doesn't matter; they can't get out." He dealt two more cards. "Pair of tens, your bet."

The doctor bet two counters, hardly looking at his cards, and came out with what had been on his mind.

"I wonder if the noise we heard had anything to do with Kaneshiro?"

"I didn't put him in there for a rest cure." Rossi dealt again, flipping the cards face up with a crisp, snapping sound. "Last card up, still your bet." The doctor complied. "The old gook was sort of a buddy of yours, wasn't he?"

"He wasn't a bad sort. We got along all right. I wish you hadn't put him in the cage. After all, it seems to me that Swenson was just as much to blame."

"Here's the one you've been waiting for." The last card came, face down. This time the doctor made his bet without being reminded. Rossi raised him a quarter.

"It's yours." The doctor turned over the cards that were showing.

"Goddammit," Rossi said, "you had me beat on the board." He turned over his hole cards and showed only a small pair. "Your deal."

The doctor took the cards and began to shuffle them; then he put them down. "I can't keep my mind on the game," he admitted. "What do I owe you?"

Rossi counted the chips remaining in front of the doctor. "Eighty-five cents. I'll add it to your account. I wish Witherspoon hadn't crapped out; we need a new man in this game."

They both turned and glanced at Witherspoon. His feet, still stockinged, were visible through the opening between the two rooms of the hut.

"Let him sleep," the doctor said. "I wish I could fall asleep like that."

"You're worrying about the stockade, aren't you?" Rossi asked. He picked up the cards and dealt himself two pat hands.

"I can't say I like it," the doctor said. "You didn't have to handle it that way."

"It'll keep the others from getting out of hand. The old gook himself will have a rough time, but it'll be something he'll remember."

"What about the others who were involved? Kaneshiro wasn't the only one, you know."

"They've disappeared. Oh, they're in the stockade all right, but it's too big for us to have any chance of finding them. Not that it matters. As long as Kaneshiro is locked up the others won't make any trouble."

"When are you going to let Kaneshiro out?"

"Later," Rossi said. "When the gooks have forgotten about him. They're scared now and that's good; I want them to be scared. But they're touchy as hell and Kaneshiro is the one gook who can make trouble for us. I'm going to leave him in there until nobody gives a damn if he's alive or dead."

Rossi played with the cards, dealing hands to himself and then shuffling the deck and dealing again. The doctor watched, silent but obviously wanting to talk. At last he spoke. "How do you know you won't wait until it's too late?"

"Too late? What for?"

"The lunatics may hurt the old man. Even if they don't, there's the possibility that he might crack up."

"Stop worrying about the old gook," Rossi said.

"If it were daylight, I'd go up and have a look. I didn't like that noise."

"Why don't you go ahead? You've been in the stockade at night before."

"No," the doctor said, "I'd just as soon not be alone in there tonight. Couldn't you have one of the guards check the cage?"

Rossi shook his head but the doctor persisted and, to his surprise, Rossi gave in. He went to the window and called for Swenson.

At sundown Swenson had been permitted to dismiss the working party. His face was puffy and streaked with sweat and dirt and his body was stiff and sore when he came through the gate. After he had eaten, the doctor had dressed his wounds while he lay stretched out on his cot. Mike was already asleep, but Swenson lay awake long after the doctor had gone.

"Let it go," the doctor said. "Swenson's had a rough day already. If you can't send anyone else, let it go until to-morrow."

"No, it won't do Swenson any harm." Rossi called Swenson again. Soon Swenson appeared in the doorway.

"What the hell's been going on?" Rossi demanded.

"The crazy gee-sha? She's just sounding off a bit early to-night. Nothing I can do about it."

"What about all this shooting? It seems to me that somebody lets off a round about every five minutes."

"The boys are sort of nervous tonight. They all get trigger-happy after they've heard a couple of shots. Once you think you're seeing Japs in the dark nobody's going to change your mind for you. The next relief'll probably be better."

"The doctor and I've been wondering what's been going on up at the cage. How do you think your friend Kaneshiro's making out?"

"That bastard can rot up there for all I care."

"I want you to go and have a look at the cage."

"I'll check it as soon as it gets light."

"No," Rossi said, "I want you to go check it now."

"For Christ's sake, Lieutenant," Swenson protested, "I'll break my goddamn neck stumbling around there in the dark."

"The dark doesn't seem to have kept you out of there before

this. Look here, Swenson, you're in trouble. I could have you broken to a goddamn private if I wanted to."

Swenson was not at all dismayed by the threat. "Hell, Lieutenant, I almost wish you would."

"Get the hell out of here and find out what's been going on at the cage." Swenson turned and started out of the door but Rossi called to him to wait. "Take Mike along with you."

"I'll break out the whole platoon if you want me to," Swenson offered.

"Just you two will be enough."

Rossi watched from the window. The light of a candle flickered in the window of Swenson's hut and illuminated the trees outside with a pale radiance. Mike, tired and angry, stood for a moment in front of the window, pulling on his dungarees. Then the light went out and Rossi heard the two men walk toward the stockade. There was no other sound except an insect buzzing that came from the trees and Witherspoon's regular breathing. The gate creaked on its hinges and then clattered shut. Rossi went back to his seat and waited.

The doctor took Rossi's place at the window. A shadow of annoyance passed over Rossi's face. "What's the matter now?" Rossi asked. "You wanted to find out what happened at the cage. Now you'll know."

"I suppose I'm worried about what they may find."

"Why should that bother you? If the old man's alive, that's what you wanted to know. If he's gone off his rocker, why then he's where he ought to be. If he's dead, that's an end to it."

"No," the doctor said, "I'm afraid that whatever happened tonight it won't be an end to it."

"We'll see," Rossi said. "How about another hand?"

186

"No, I've had enough." But the doctor sat down and watched he cards that Rossi was dealing to himself.

"I'd never deal myself hands like that in a game," Rossi said, icking up a full house, pat. "Come on, I'll deal you in this ime." He began to deal cards to the doctor, but the doctor icked them up and turned them over.

"I don't feel like it. Go on playing by yourself."

Rossi brought the deck together neatly and slapped it own.

"You're being pretty stupid about this gook. Two days ago ou said you didn't like the way I was running the stockade. ou were right; it was in a hell of a mess. My men were running ild and so were the gooks. It was all my own goddamn fault. had to do something and I had to do it fast. I think it's orked. Kaneshiro was the worst of the troublemakers, but ow he's out of the way. Swenson and Mike aren't going o be looking for any more trouble. Swenson's so mad he'd robably kill the old gook himself if I'd let him. The stock-de's quiet, and I think it'll last until we pull out of here. You ay not like the way I've gone about it, but you have to admit nat it's done the trick."

The doctor made a final effort to communicate his fears to Rossi. "You don't have to let the old man die. You've stopped he trouble in your platoon and you've put the fear of God nto the prisoners — I'll grant you all that, but I'm not sure ou aren't running the risk of stirring up more trouble than ou've put down. You used to be able to control the stockade nrough Kaneshiro. If he dies all you'll have left are your uns."

"That's the way I want it," Rossi said. "A gun is one thing gook can understand."

The doctor sighed and rocked back on his seat. "Don't for-get that there are five thousand of them and only thirty of us We could kill a lot of them but in the end they'd overwhelm us."

"I don't think there's much chance of that," Rossi said "Whose side are you on anyway?"

"I'm on yours, of course," the doctor said. "Not because I think you're necessarily in the right, not because I think you have a superior moral position, but simply because I have to count on you to get us all out of this mess."

Rossi went back to his cards, laying out two or three hand of stud at a time and betting on the most likely winner. It was a long time before they heard the sounds of Swenson and Mike returning. Their voices were raised in a brief, unintelligible conversation with the guard at the gate. Soon afterward they entered Rossi's hut.

"It ain't good at all, Lieutenant," Swenson said. "The nut got him."

"Got who?" Rossi asked, although the answer was plain

"The old gook, Kaneshiro. He looked like he was choked to death."

"Goddamn!" Rossi said, and for a moment there was silence in the room. "How about the other gooks? Did you run into any of them at all?"

"No," Swenson said, "we didn't see another gook the whole time we were in there."

Rossi got to his feet. "Come on. You, Mike, pick up a ham mer and a crowbar and meet us at the gate."

The doctor, left alone in the room with only the sleeping Witherspoon to keep him company, listened to Rossi and Swen son walking to the gate. A little later Mike's footsteps wen down the path. The gate swung open and slammed shut, creaking on both the outward and the inward swings. The doctor remained crouched over, his elbows on his knees, as if he were in pain.

Seventeen

THERE was a slight chill in the early morning air and the breeze that blew toward the mountain was fresh and smelled of the sea. Witherspoon had slept well and he walked briskly toward the gate. Rossi walked beside him and Mike limped behind.

Yamazaki, the boy who had been a gunner, was still sleeping on the bare ground, but the other four prisoners-of-war were moving around inside the square Rossi had marked off. When they saw Witherspoon they crowded to the wire and called to him in loud, cheerful voices. The listlessness they had shown on the day before seemed to have disappeared along with their masquerade as civilians.

"Your gooks look full of fight today," Rossi said.

Witherspoon smiled, pleased with the notion that these prisoners were no longer Rossi's, but his. "They say they're hungry. When can they get something to eat?"

"Tell them they'll get fed when the gooks get busy at the galley." Rossi looked toward the galley and was dissatisfied with what he saw: not only the galley but the entire square was deserted. Around the perimeter of the square, almost in the trees, a few prisoners could be seen moving about, but none of them came into the square itself. At that hour the galley should have been the center of long lines of hungry Okinawans, each impatiently waiting his turn at a steaming kettle of rice. It had been Witherspoon's plan to remove the men he wanted to question from the chow lines, saving himself and Mike a tedious journey from hut to hut.

"Ask them if they know what's going on," Rossi said.

When Witherspoon put the question to them the prisoners-of-war shook their heads; their only answer was a renewed demand for food, deferential but persistent, as if they believed that because a special interest had been taken in them they were entitled to special treatment. They carried their request to Mike in the hope that the officer had somehow misunderstood them and once the situation was properly explained there would be no question but that they would receive their breakfast.

"Tell them I can't feed them," Rossi said. "When their own people come out to make chow I'll have some sent over to them."

The corporal ordered the others to stop their grumbling and they drifted away from the wire and turned their anger toward the absent cooks. The corporal produced a cigarette butt from his shirt pocket and begged a light from Witherspoon. Witherspoon struck a match and held it to the corporal's cigarette. The corporal took a deep drag and let the smoke trickle out through his nostrils.

"Don't worry about them," the corporal said. "They're soldiers and they ought to be used to empty stomachs." He smiled but Witherspoon felt that he had been subtly rebuked for failing in his responsibility toward his prisoners.

Across the square, the doctor emerged from the trees and walked toward the gate, coming from sick bay. When he was near, Witherspoon saw that his face was troubled. He passed the prisoners-of-war without a glance and came through the gate.

"No patients again today," the doctor said. "A couple of cases in the ward have pulled out without so much as a by-your-leave. The others say their families came and took them home."

"I didn't figure they'd take it this hard," Rossi said.

"Take what hard?" Witherspoon asked. His question went unanswered. "Does it have anything to do with my interrogations?"

"No, no," the doctor said, "I don't think that bothers them particularly."

"What is it then?"

"One of the prisoners died last night," the doctor said. "It was while you were sleeping."

"Do you think they've gone into mourning for him?"

"Something of the sort," the doctor said.

Rossi and the doctor were both looking toward the galley. Witherspoon saw nothing there that was unusual. The death of an unknown prisoner didn't seem to concern him; he picked up the map case that held his paper and pencils and prepared to enter the stockade. "If I get a line on what's bothering them I'll let you know."

"Thanks," Rossi said.

The guard opened the gate and the two interpreters started toward the galley. The desk they had improvised on the rice pots had been dismantled and Witherspoon intended to set it up again before venturing in among the huts. Mike was still limping and he lagged behind so that Witherspoon arrived at the shed several paces ahead of him. Witherspoon was alone when he turned the corner of the shed.

Witherspoon recognized the object at his feet as a dead man, but in the shock of the first moment he saw the corpse in front of him less distinctly than he saw a long dark tunnel in which the bodies lay shoulder to shoulder in a foul green slime. The evil stink that had risen from the slime was momentarily as real as the paralysis that prevented Witherspoon from backing away, or even from withdrawing his foot from contact with one of the dead man's hands.

Mike's unimpassioned voice dispersed the images of the cave. "I should have warned you."

The spell broken, Witherspoon retreated a step and for the first time saw clearly what was in front of him. The corpse had been dropped carelessly on the ground so that its limbs sprawled unnaturally in the dust. The old, wrinkled, agonized face lay in the shade thrown by a board that had been driven into the ground. On the board, in hastily written Japanese characters, were the words: THIS MAN DIED BECAUSE HE ATTACKED A UNITED STATES MARINE. A fly alighted on the dead man's mouth and strolled casually over the cracked lips.

"How did this get here?"

"Lieutenant Rossi wanted it here."

"Who was it?"

"Kaneshiro," Mike told him. "He was the headman."

Witherspoon remembered the doctor's story of Mike and Swenson's abortive raid on the Okinawans' liquor supply. "I suppose you're pretty pleased with yourself," Witherspoon said, his habitual diffidence overcome by an unaccustomed quickening of indignation.

"Kaneshiro was a crooked old son of a bitch," Mike said, "but I didn't want this to happen. I didn't want any part in this whole business."

Witherspoon turned from the corpse and started for the gate,

193

a hot pulse of anger beating in his temples. His sense of outrage was strengthened by the knowledge that here at last, after the humiliation of the cave, he was right and Rossi was wrong.

Rossi and the doctor were still at the gate. When Witherspoon came closer he knew from their faces that they were both prepared for what he was going to say. Aware of Witherspoon's agitation, the prisoners-of-war rocked back on their heels and looked on curiously.

"What's that corpse doing in there?" To Witherspoon's dismay, his voice had taken on an unfamiliar reedy quality.

"I wanted it where all the gooks could see it."

"Why?" Again his voice sounded thin and unsteady, like that of a schoolboy arguing with a teacher.

"I think it's the best way to handle the gooks."

"Well, I don't and I think you'd better get it out of there."

"I'll take it out when I'm ready." Witherspoon found that he had nothing more to say. Rossi said quietly, "I'm running this stockade, Witherspoon."

Witherspoon uttered a threat that, even as he spoke, he knew to be rhetorical. "When Division hears about this you may take a different view of it."

"I'll take a chance on that," Rossi said and turned his back and left.

The doctor, who had remained silent during the exchange between Witherspoon and Rossi, stayed at the gate.

"What are we going to do?" Witherspoon asked him.

"Nothing," the doctor said.

"But we can't leave it in there!"

"I'm afraid we're going to have to." The doctor spoke in a tone of quiet resignation. Witherspoon tried one more question.

"Why?"

"Lieutenant Rossi's in charge of this stockade," the doctor said. There was no mockery in his voice. He turned around and followed Rossi away from the stockade.

Witherspoon looked back toward the galley and saw that Mike was coming, bringing the map case with him. The prisoners-of-war looked curiously from Witherspoon to Mike and then beyond Mike to the galley where Kaneshiro's body was hidden from their view.

Witherspoon put his hand on the gate and shook it. "Open it up," he said. "I'm coming out."

When Witherspoon reached the hut and sat down on his cot he was shaking. He found a quarter of an inch of rum in the bottom of the doctor's last bottle and drank it. It helped the trembling of his body but did nothing to quiet the agitation of his mind. Mike came in and put the map case on the cot.

"I guess there's no point in trying to talk to them today," Mike said.

"No," Witherspoon said, "not today."

"You know, that old bastard tried to kill me but I still don't like this business."

"Lieutenant Rossi's running this stockade," Witherspoon said bitterly. "You'd better watch what you say, Mike."

"Shit," Mike said, and left.

After Mike had gone the doctor came in. He took off his boots and stretched out on his cot as if he were going to try to sleep. Instead, he lay there for a long time with his eyes open. Witherspoon stayed in the room even though he found the doctor's calmness almost unbearably irritating.

"Why don't you go back to Division?" the doctor asked after a while.

"I may," Witherspoon said.

"You're not going to make things any easier for yourself by fighting with Rossi. Take the prisoners you have now and come back when Rossi's gone."

"If I go back to Division it won't be to wait until Rossi's gone. I'll do everything I can to kick up a stink about this situation. I don't think Colonel Smith's going to be as casual about this as you seem to be."

"I'm not being casual," the doctor said. He remained on his back, apparently relaxed, but there was a telltale shrillness in his voice. "I'm sick about this whole business. I'm sick to the point of not knowing how I'm going to stick it out much longer. If I could leave here, Witherspoon, I'd get out so fast you wouldn't see me for the smoke. And I'd spend the rest of my life trying to forget the things that have happened to me at this goddamn stockade."

The doctor raised himself on an elbow so that he could look at Witherspoon. "The last twist of the knife is your youthful certainty that if you just mean well and bull your way ahead everything will turn out all right. If I had the slightest faith that we could accomplish anything I'd say go ahead and have it out with Rossi. But I know that all we'd succeed in doing would be to make things worse than they are now."

"It seems to me that we have to try."

"We've already tried. If I were you I'd get in my jeep and get the hell out of here. I have to stay, but you're just an innocent bystander. You're not really mixed up in this mess."

"I seem to be getting more mixed up in it every day." As an afterthought Witherspoon added, "Even if I decide to go, it won't be because I'm running away."

"Have it your own way," the doctor said. "But if you decide to stay don't expect me to be on your side."

"I won't," Witherspoon promised, and left the hut.

Witherspoon found Corcoran working on their jeep. Corcoran was sprawled across a fender; he wasn't aware of Witherspoon's presence until he lifted his head to reach for a socket wrench.

"I'm thinking of going back to Division," Witherspoon said. "How soon can you get this machine rolling?"

"Give me half an hour."

"What's the matter with it? It was running all right yesterday."

Corcoran looked around with mock furtiveness and spoke in a hoarse whisper. "That half-ass sergeant tried to put me to work. I figured I'd better get busy on something." Corcoran flattened himself out on the fender again. He came up for air in a minute and wiped away a long smear of grease along his cheekbone. "What's the trouble in there?"

"The prisoners are acting up," Witherspoon said, seeing no need for going into a fuller explanation.

"I guess the gooks don't like that stiff in there," Corcoran said.

"How did you find out about it?"

Corcoran motioned with his wrench toward Swenson's hut. "That jerk of a sergeant was talking about it last night. It looks like they've really screwed up the works, doesn't it?"

"It doesn't look good," Witherspoon agreed.

Corcoran went back to work. Witherspoon watched him wrestle with a balky nut. "The colonel's not going to like it," Corcoran said. "If I were you, Lieutenant, I wouldn't go back until I'd caught a few more Japs for him."

Witherspoon grunted to show that he had heard.

"Maybe this isn't any of my business, Lieutenant, but if you let Lieutenant Rossi run you out of here you'll spend the rest of your life getting run out of places." Witherspoon didn't answer immediately and Corcoran said, "I guess I'm talking out of turn."

"No," Witherspoon said, "you're not talking out of turn at all."

Swenson and Mike were at the gate. They were passing out picks and shovels to the prisoners-of-war, who looked as if they were still hungry.

"I've been looking all over for you, Lieutenant," Swenson said, although it was plain that his search could not have taken him out of sight of the gate. "We're going to have to use your gooks today." He handed a shovel to Yamazaki and added belatedly, "If that's all right with you."

"What happened to the working party you had yesterday?"

"They've taken off somewhere. We'll fix their wagon when we catch them, but Lieutenant Rossi says we got to get ahead with the well."

"I don't mind your putting them to work," Witherspoon said, "but I don't want to take any chances on losing them."

"They won't get away," Swenson assured him. He twirled his club and clouted an imaginary prisoner. "The first one that makes a break is going to get his goddamn head broken."

Mike lined the prisoners up in a single file. "Why don't you come along, Lieutenant?"

Witherspoon didn't relish the prospect of spending the day in the hut with the doctor, nor did he want to wander around the stockade, running the risk of an unexpected encounter with

Rossi. He would be ready to face Rossi later, not now. Consequently, he fell in at the end of the little procession that started across the deserted square.

At first, Kaneshiro's body was hidden by the galley but it soon came into view, first the feet and legs, then the body, and finally the sign at Kaneshiro's head, illegible in the distance. The prisoners craned their necks to stare at the body but, except for the youngest prisoner, they said nothing.

"That was Kaneshiro, wasn't it?" Yamazaki asked Mike.

"That's right."

"He was in the cage with the lunatics, wasn't he?"

"Yes."

"They killed him last night."

"Yes."

"That was what you were doing in the stockade."

Mike said nothing.

"Well," the boy said, "he was an old fool, anyway."

When the working party was almost in the shade of the trees Witherspoon saw a girl walk into the empty square.

"Look," he said to Swenson, "it's the first Okinawan I've seen today."

"It's Peggy," Swenson said. He called for Mike to stop and they all turned to watch the girl run toward the galley. She stumbled once and picked herself up and ran on until she reached Kaneshiro's body. Witherspoon heard muffled sobs as she knelt by her uncle's body.

"His niece," Yamazaki said, and leered at Swenson.

"Wipe that goddamn grin off your face," Swenson bellowed, and the boy promptly turned away. "Come on, let's get going."

"You called her Peggy," Witherspoon said.

"She was a good kid," Swenson said.

As they filed up the path the Okinawans in the courtyards watched them sullenly. The prisoners-of-war began to talk among themselves but Swenson ordered them to knock it off before Witherspoon had caught the sense of their remarks. The prisoners now walked with their eyes straight ahead, not from embarrassment, but from the old ingrained disdain of the Japanese soldier for the Okinawan civilian.

"The Okinawans don't look very cheerful," Witherspoon said to Swenson.

Swenson looked at the unrevealing faces of a group of old men who were watching them. "They're pissed off about Kaneshiro."

They were almost at the well when Witherspoon spoke again. "Don't you ever worry about being mobbed when you're inside the stockade?"

"I never worry about that. The first day we were here I walked through the square by myself with nothing but my club."

"You couldn't stop them if they ganged up on you."

"They won't," Swenson said confidently.

They left the last of the huts behind them and entered a clearing which had been beaten smooth by the feet of thousands of women carrying water buckets. The well itself was now only a deep, irregularly-shaped depression in the middle of the clearing. It was surrounded by mounds of raw yellow earth that had been heaped up by the previous working party. The hoist that Swenson had erected, a great tripod of heavy beams, straddled the well.

Swenson wasted no time in putting the prisoners to work. On the day before, the working party had uncovered a boulder that lay squarely across the shaft. Swenson sent two of the prisoners into the mud at the bottom of the well to secure a rope around the boulder, but he quickly grew impatient with their progress and descended the shaft himself.

Witherspoon remained on the surface with the others. Mike and the three Japanese stood around the mouth of the well but Witherspoon was soon bored with the operation at the bottom of the shaft. He looked up and saw a woman half hidden in the trees at the edge of the clearing. When she saw that Witherspoon had seen her she came into the open. She was taller and slimmer than most of the Okinawan women but she wore the farm woman's uniform of blouse and pantaloons. Her gaunt face was streaked with caked dust and her hair was pulled back in an untidy knot. Not until she raised her arm and beckoned to him did Witherspoon recognize the Madame.

None of the men at the well were aware of Witherspoon's leaving. He hurried across the clearing, wondering about the message that the Madame was unwilling to deliver in the hearing of the others. When he came closer he saw that the gauntness of her face was caused by fear. She clutched Witherspoon by the arm and drew him into the shade of the trees. She began to speak; the words rushed out like a cataract. There was no staying her; she pleaded, cajoled, threatened, and cried out in sheer exasperation, but Witherspoon, unable to cope with her fluency, understood hardly a word.

Mike heard the Madame's voice and came toward them. The Madame watched him warily, her fingers tightening on Witherspoon's wrist.

"What do you want?" Mike asked.

At that very moment Swenson secured the line around the boulder to his satisfaction. His voice roared from the depths of the well, "I said *pull!* Goddammit, what's going on up there?"

The Madame hesitated, torn between the urgency of her message and her fear of Swenson. Then Swenson's head appeared over one of the mounds of earth. The Madame released Witherspoon's wrist and fled into the trees.

Neither Mike nor Witherspoon ever found out what it was that the Madame had wanted to tell them.

Eighteen

ROSSI was rubbing thin cold-water suds over his wrists and hands when Witherspoon called to him from the back window of the hut. Rossi turned from the cistern, the water dripping from the tips of his fingers.

"If the men have any chow left over I'd like to give it to the prisoners," Witherspoon said.

Rossi turned back to the cistern and went on washing; his voice came back to Witherspoon slightly attenuated, as if by the act of turning his back Rossi had removed himself to a greater distance. "Go ahead, just as long as you don't let them out of the cage."

Outside the door of the hut the doctor was blowing on some scraps of kindling under the charcoal in the earthenware cooking stove. It was the opening move of his customary evening ritual. The simple motions of preparing dinner seemed to give him relief from the strain of the day's work and neither Witherspoon nor Rossi had had any cause to complain of his cooking.

"Don't be long," the doctor said. "It'll be ready in fifteen or twenty minutes." Nothing in his manner showed that he remembered his earlier conversation with Witherspoon.

Witherspoon nodded to him and crossed the yard to Swenson's hut. The square could be seen from the yard between the huts; it was still deserted except for the prisoners-of-war just inside the fence. Four of the Japanese were sitting with their backs against the wire, facing the square. They sat close together, as if they were trying to draw the greatest measure of companionship from each other's presence. Yamazaki alone stayed apart, singing a song Witherspoon had heard before, a nostalgic air extolling the beauty of the nights in China. The boy's slight voice was almost lost in the silence of the stockade.

Mike took Witherspoon into the lee of the barracks shed, where they found a couple of inches of stew cooling in the bottom of an iron pot like those at the galley in the stockade. Mike ladled the stew into a large tin can he had brought with him.

"You know, Lieutenant," he said, "these guys like Swenson are all crazy. They think the Jap soldiers we caught are all right: they work hard and they don't make any trouble. But you'd think the Okinawans all belonged to the Black Dragon Society or something."

"You and Swenson didn't help things any," Witherspoon pointed out.

"We were damn fools," Mike said. He went into the shed. When he came back some spoons had been tucked into his pocket. "What a hell of a screwed-up situation this has turned into!" He picked up the can and swirled it to break up the thin scum of pink grease that was forming on the surface. "Somebody ought to beat some sense into Lieutenant Rossi's head."

"You'd better leave Lieutenant Rossi to me," Witherspoon said.

"I'll be glad to leave him to you, Lieutenant, but what can you do?"

"I've had a couple of ideas," Witherspoon said.

Mike put down the can and looked with surprise at Witherspoon. "You're going to do something?"

Witherspoon had not intended to reveal his plan to anyone; as long as it was only in his mind he was free to modify it, to temporize, or to withdraw entirely. Now, almost by accident, he was fully committed.

"Can you stay at the gate for a couple of hours after we finish feeding the prisoners?"

"Sure, Lieutenant."

"This may get you in a jam," Witherspoon warned him. "If it does, I won't be in a position to do you any good."

"I'll take a chance," Mike said. He didn't ask any more questions. Witherspoon had the impression that it was because he didn't need to. "You go get your chow, Lieutenant. I'll take care of the Japs."

The doctor was bending over the stove, stirring a mixture of ham and pineapple from one of the cans in the ten-in-one rations. Rossi was still at the cistern. Witherspoon sat down to wait for his dinner.

"So you've decided to stay," the doctor said.

"There didn't seem to be much point in going back after all," Witherspoon said. "For one thing, I would have caught hell from the colonel for not bringing back more prisoners."

The doctor stirred the food as carefully as if there were nothing on his mind more important than browning the ham evenly. So off-handedly that it might have been a comment on the weather, he asked, "Are you still set on having Rossi take Kaneshiro's body out of the stockade?"

"Yes." Witherspoon, guarding his secret, was equally casual.

"Why don't you let it go? It doesn't matter very much if it stays there for another day or not."

"It matters to me," Witherspoon said, masking the seriousness of his answer with an apologetic smile.

"You know where I stand. If you start a fight with Rossi, don't expect any help from me. I've washed my hands of the whole business." The doctor speared a morsel of pineapple on a tine of his fork. "I've washed my hands of it," he repeated, nibbling delicately at the pineapple.

Witherspoon found the doctor's self-possession all the more offensive because he knew it was as counterfeit as his own. After a moment's silence he said, "There's something you ought to keep in mind. When your military government team shows up here you may have a hard time explaining to them why the dead man was none of your business."

The doctor grimaced wryly. "You're trying to blackmail me."

"Call it anything you like, you're still going to have to do a lot of fast talking."

The doctor shrugged. "I'll worry about that when the time comes."

"A lot of things may happen before then." The doctor didn't say anything and Witherspoon goaded him with a final question. "Are you afraid of Rossi?"

The doctor looked Witherspoon full in the face. "Yes, I'm afraid. Aren't you?"

Witherspoon was spared from having to answer by Rossi's arrival. Rossi was wearing the same dungarees he had worn all day, but he had shaved and his hair was slick with water.

"How does the stockade look tonight?" Rossi asked Witherspoon.

"Pretty quiet. The Okinawans haven't come back to the square yet."

"They'll be back soon," Rossi said confidently. "I wouldn't be surprised if you could get back to work tomorrow."

"I hope so."

The doctor took the pan from the fire and divided the contents among three porcelain rice bowls.

"Maybe we'll get you in on our poker game after all," Rossi said.

Witherspoon smiled but said nothing. They took up their rice bowls and began to eat. Rossi stowed away his food until his bowl was clean. Witherspoon and the doctor picked at their food and put their bowls away only half empty. The doctor set a kettle of water to boil and opened a can of powdered coffee and a tin of condensed milk.

"What were you doing with yourself all day?" Rossi asked Witherspoon. "I didn't see you after you came out of the stockade this morning."

Witherspoon told him about the well and the Madame's furtive visit. Rossi frowned. "It wouldn't have been a bad idea if I'd put her in the cage along with Kaneshiro."

"She won't be giving you any more trouble. I've never seen a woman as frightened as she was."

Rossi grunted; Witherspoon started at the sound as if it had been a cue for which he had been waiting. It was important to him to say the things he had to say in just the way he had rehearsed them in his mind. He went inside to light the lantern he had brought from Division. Rossi and the doctor followed him, bringing the canteen cups full of coffee.

As soon as they had sat down, Witherspoon said, "I imagine you've wondered why I didn't go back to Division." Rossi looked politely curious. Witherspoon went on, "I'll tell you why: I intend to see that you take Kaneshiro's body out of the stockade."

The doctor gulped at the hot coffee, burned his mouth and sucked in a cooling draft of air. "Damn!" he said softly.

"I thought we'd been through all that already," Rossi said, setting his cup on the floor.

"I'm going to ask you once more."

"No," Rossi said.

It was the answer Witherspoon had expected, but he deliberately delayed revealing his intention.

"Ask the doctor what he thinks."

"I don't give a good goddamn what the doctor thinks," Rossi said, but his voice was patient and it was clear that he meant the statement not hostilely but as a simple declaration of fact. The doctor, relieved at having been spared, ran his fingers through his thin hair.

Witherspoon persisted, unwilling to let the doctor escape so easily. "Tell Rossi what you think, Doctor."

Rossi fixed the doctor in a steady gaze and waited for his answer. "It's none of my business," the doctor said. "You're running the stockade, Rossi." But he flinched when his eyes met Witherspoon's and he turned away, the depletion of his spirit showing as clearly in his hunched, flabby body as in his face. He gestured vaguely to show that he could not have said anything else.

Rossi's voice was no longer patient. He spoke with a sort of exasperated finality. "If the gooks turn out for breakfast tomorrow morning I'll take it out. Otherwise it stays where it is."

"Very well," Witherspoon said. He crossed the room and

208

picked up a flashlight that was lying next to the carbine on Rossi's cot. "If you won't do it, I will."

Instead of leaving immediately, he waited, hoping that his determination would move Rossi to relent. Later he realized that it was at that moment that he lost control of the events of the night. The dialogue he had rehearsed gave out and what happened afterward was tainted with lunatic unreality, as if he had had thrust into his hands a script written by a cunning idiot.

"Oh, for Christ's sake!" Rossi reached for the flashlight but Witherspoon snatched it away from him and backed toward the door.

"Don't try to stop me," Witherspoon warned Rossi, but Rossi walked toward him with the wariness of a man trying to capture a dog that had slipped its leash. Witherspoon backed down the steps.

Rossi, framed in the doorway, spoke. "If you go through with this I'm going to send you back to Division under guard."

Witherspoon flashed the light tauntingly in Rossi's eyes. "If I leave here it won't be because anyone ran me out." The words echoed in his consciousness like something said by somebody else, as false and hollow as his voice was shrill and unconvincing. He turned his back and walked toward the stockade.

He was halted by Rossi's voice, calling after him. "Hold on!" He turned and saw Rossi in the window. "I can't keep you from making a damn fool of yourself but I can't afford to let you get killed. I'm going to send Swenson in with you."

"I don't need Swenson," Witherspoon said obstinately. "I don't want any help from you or any of your men." But Swenson was already coming from his hut in answer to Rossi's summons.

"Lieutenant Witherspoon is going into the stockade to get Kaneshiro's body. I want you to go with him. You can take the Jap prisoners to dig the grave."

"Okay," Swenson said. "You want him buried inside the stockade?"

"Somewhere near the wire will do. You can put the sign up for a marker."

Compelled by Rossi's matter-of-fact manner and Swenson's inescapable presence, Witherspoon permitted the sergeant to accompany him. He was, as a matter of fact, relieved that the actual execution of the burial had been taken out of his hands. Swenson prudently didn't talk; it was clear to him that there had been a dispute between the two officers in which he would be wise not to meddle.

The yellow beam of the flashlight picked out Mike, sitting outside the gate with the guard, Davis.

"What the hell are you doing?" Swenson asked.

"Just banging ears with Davis," Mike said, but he lifted the bolt across the gate before Witherspoon had said anything about going inside.

The prisoners-of-war complained peevishly when Mike told them to pick up the shovels they had used at the well. Yamazaki protested in a comically intended falsetto that he was too full of stew to move.

Witherspoon brusquely urged them to come along. He was anxious now to finish the job and started toward the galley. The flashlight emitted a pale beam that lighted up a narrow path ahead of them that was like a catwalk spanning a dark abyss over which they hurried to reach the shed at the far end.

As if they had suddenly emerged from a fog, the light picked out the galley. Witherspoon stopped short. A great crowd, their backs toward the burial party, surrounded the shed, blocking the path to Kaneshiro's body. Witherspoon felt Swenson's hand on his arm.

"Easy, Lieutenant."

The crowd turned. It was, of course, only the Okinawans.

"Let's go," Swenson said confidently. In the rear Mike urged on the prisoners-of-war and they started forward again with Swenson swinging his club in the lead. When they came closer the light picked out the familiar figures: wiry old men, women of all ages, and the children who before the trouble began were accustomed to play all day in the square. Swenson chanted in a good-humored bullying voice, "Break it up, break it up, you gooks, let's break it up and go home." Mike's voice took up the cry in Japanese.

The Okinawans pressed together in a more compact mass but they held their ground when the burial party drove them back against the shed. "Break it up, break it up," Swenson repeated, moving toward the Okinawans with his club poised to stab at a belly or crack a wrist.

Witherspoon's nostrils were filled with a rank, penetrating smell, a fetid distillation of bodily secretions which might have come from the burrow of an enormous animal. The short hairs along Witherspoon's spine prickled and he was reminded that a dog is said to detect the smell of fear streaming from the pores of a frightened human being.

The circle of Okinawans surged forward; it was a terrifyingly purposeful movement, the defensive reaction of a single living thing controlled by a single primitive brain.

"Stop!" Witherspoon shouted, begging for time in which to explain why he had come. It was not that he was frightened; in a singularly detached way he marveled at his own composure.

"Wait!" he cried, but the Okinawans continued to come at him.

Swenson struck out with his club, forcing a path through the dense mass of bodies. The others, carrying Witherspoon along with them, rushed behind Swenson, the prisoners-of-war fending off the Okinawans with their shovels. They drove through the outer ranks toward the heart of the great stinking beast. A bare hand touched Witherspoon's face for an instant like the palp of a sea animal feeling out the shape of an intruder. There was a scream and the Okinawans surged forward again, expelling the intruders from their midst.

Swenson's voice said hoarsely, "Want to try it again, Lieutenant?"

Witherspoon turned the light on him. Swenson angrily pushed Witherspoon's arm aside so that the light pointed off into the square, but in the moment the light had shone on him Witherspoon had seen the look on Swenson's face, a look not of fear but of complete and overwhelming surprise. "Turn that goddamn light off," Swenson ordered. "You want them to jump us?"

"I'm sorry," Witherspoon said, switching the light off. They remained in the darkness facing the Okinawans for only a moment longer. Then Mike called out what was in all their minds, "Let's get the hell out of here!"

The first thing Rossi asked was if the body were still in the stockade. Witherspoon told him that they hadn't been able to find out because of the Okinawans.

"You're not going to let the gooks scare you out, are you?"

Swenson spoke up. "We're trying to tell you, Lieutenant, the

212

gooks aren't going to let us through. There's just too many of them. Even if you knock some of them out of the way, there's still a couple of hundred between you and the galley."

"Are you scared too, Charley?" Rossi asked mockingly.

"You know damn well I'm not scared. But I'm telling you this, Lieutenant: You're not going to get anywhere until you go in with weapons. There just ain't no use going back there otherwise."

Instead of welcoming the abortive end of Witherspoon's undertaking, Rossi seemed to have found a new reason for forcing it to its planned conclusion. Nothing more was said about sending Witherspoon to Division under guard. Instead, Rossi said, "This was your idea, Witherspoon, and you can damn well see it through. Take as many men as you want. Swenson'll know what to do."

Witherspoon realized that he had been so thoroughly beaten that there was no choice left to him but outright retreat. "The morning will be soon enough," he said.

"You're sure of that?" Rossi asked.

"Yes, I'm sure." Witherspoon sat down and lowered his head into his hands. "You son of a bitch," he said softly.

Rossi smiled, almost regretfully. "That's all, Charley." Swenson left to go to the gate where Mike was waiting with the prisoners-of-war.

Witherspoon came into the bright circle of light thrown by the lantern and gathered up the notes he had made during the interrogation of the prisoners. He sat by the lantern and painstakingly went through his papers, trying to suppress the image of the monstrous thing that had confronted him in the stockade. It was no use. His only victory had been that he had not been afraid, and now it seemed a poor sort of victory. He knew

213

that he would never escape from the consequences of his discovery that good will and compassion and humaneness had not been enough.

Rossi took his carbine from where it hung on the wall and broke it down to clean it. Even in his distraught state Witherspoon was comforted by the knowledge that Rossi, too, was taking refuge from his thoughts in a familiar ritual. From the next room came the creak of wood and canvas as the doctor tossed on his cot.

Witherspoon went on with his work even after the geisha had begun to sing. It was her familiar serenade, a crazy howling that was somewhere between a song and the cry of an animal. To Witherspoon it seemed but one more mocking comment on his failure. The geisha's voice broke off abruptly but her song was taken up by another voice in the stockade. It became a plaintive lament that rose to a high, piercing climax and then fell off into quiet sobbing.

Rossi went to the window and Witherspoon followed, drawn unwillingly by the weird sounds from the stockade. They searched the darkness but all it yielded was Swenson, who appeared in the shaft of light that was thrown from the window.

"What the hell is it now?" Rossi asked.

"It sounds like one of the gooks by the galley. Mike's keeping an eye on them." Swenson came into the hut.

The wailing rose again. The first voice had been joined by others, and even as Witherspoon listened, the cry grew stronger and became charged with grief. The doctor, blinking in the light, entered the room. He sat down and rubbed his face with the palms of his hands. While the mournful keening continued they remained as they were: Swenson just inside the door, Witherspoon and Rossi by the window, and the doctor seated.

"We'll have to put a stop to that," Rossi said.

"There's nothing you can do about it," the doctor said. "My God, Rossi, are you going to try to stop them from mourning for a dead man?"

One group of voices rose to an unbearably high and penetrating shriek, which was suddenly cut off, only to be followed immediately by another chorus taking up the burden of the lament. The rise and fall became regular, each chorus growing in strength over the preceding one until the flood of sound undulated like a succession of waves beating on a shore.

"Go in there and shut them up, Charley," Rossi said. He spoke quietly, with the unshakable self-confidence of a man whose orders had never been disobeyed.

"No," Swenson said.

The wailing broke from the bounds of the square and spread until the whole stockade seemed to have united in a single chorus. It was suddenly clear to Witherspoon that the Okinawans were not merely mourning the incarceration and death of Kaneshiro; more important than that was their bewildered, inarticulate anger at everything the battle for the island had done to them. Witherspoon knew that their accusation was directed against him as much as against any of the other men in the room. The doctor had been right — there had never been any choice, for Witherspoon was, and had always been, on Rossi's side. Rossi was in command and in the end the only rebel was the least expected one, Swenson.

Rossi turned his head away from the window so that the lantern threw grotesque shadows across his face. "No?"

"No. I don't feel like killing gooks tonight, Lieutenant."

Rossi, walking deliberately and in full command of himself, crossed the room to his cot and picked up his carbine, which was gleaming with a light coat of fresh oil. He swung toward the door; not until that instant did Witherspoon realize fully what Rossi was about to do. He saw Rossi coming toward him on the way to the door and then he himself did something that redeemed a small measure of the self-respect he had lost in the cave and this very night in the stockade. When Rossi was almost abreast of him Witherspoon sprang forward to block the way to the door, throwing himself like a football player at Rossi's body, but Rossi twisted agilely out of the way and with a thrust of his carbine butt sent Witherspoon to the floor, clutching at his belly.

Doubled up on the floor, Witherspoon heard Rossi's footsteps going down the path toward the stockade. The gate creaked open and then there were other footsteps outside the hut as Swenson ran after Rossi. The wailing almost died out. A moment later it broke out louder than before.

Somewhere in the room behind Witherspoon the doctor moaned, "Oh God! Oh my God!"

Witherspoon picked himself off the floor and ran toward the gate. The path that was so familiar in the daylight had become treacherous in the darkness. He tripped and lurched into a tree, striking his head against the thick corky bark.

While he was leaning against the tree, fighting the sourness that welled up from his stomach, he heard the flat report of a carbine. The wailing rose to a high point. An anguished shriek hung on the air. Then there was silence.

Davis had stayed at his post at the gate. When Witherspoon came up to him he put his hand on Witherspoon's arm and said, "He wouldn't be stopped; how could I have stopped him?"

Witherspoon shook off Davis's detaining hand and entered the stockade. Swenson and Mike, running toward the galley, were silhouetted against the beam of their own flashlight. The Okinawans were gone. Swenson and Mike disappeared in the darkness behind the galley.

When Witherspoon turned the corner of the shed he saw Rossi lying on the ground. Kaneshiro's body was gone. Rossi's carbine lay near him; Witherspoon could see the smear of blood on the stock. Swenson held the flashlight while Mike, kneeling on the ground, lifted Rossi's head from the dust and turned his face into the light. There was no question then that it was all over.

Witherspoon and Mike together picked up Rossi's body and started toward the gate. Swenson led the way, carrying the flashlight and Rossi's carbine. They went slowly at first, cradling the body gently, but they began to run when they heard the geisha's voice. She was singing a wild, triumphant song that pursued them like a hot wind as they fled from the stockade.